SEALED WITH A DISS

SEALED WITH A DISS

A CLIQUE NOVEL BY
LISI HARRISON

poppy

LITTLE, BROWN AND COMPANY
New York   Boston

Poppy

Little, Brown and Company
Hachette Book Group USA
237 Park Avenue, New York, NY 10017
For more of your favorite series, go to www.pickapoppy.com

First Edition: July 2007

The Poppy name and logo are trademarks of Hachette Book Group USA.

Cover photo by Roger Moenks • Author photo by Gillian Crane
Cover design by Andrea C. Uva and Sarah Kearney

alloyentertainment

Produced by Alloy Entertainment
151 West 26th Street, New York, NY 10001

ISBN-10: 0-316-11506-1
ISBN-13: 978-0-316-11506-3

10 9 8 7 6 5
CWO
Printed in the United States of America

CLIQUE novels by Lisi Harrison:

THE CLIQUE
BEST FRIENDS FOR NEVER
REVENGE OF THE WANNABES
INVASION OF THE BOY SNATCHERS
THE PRETTY COMMITTEE STRIKES BACK
DIAL L FOR LOSER
IT'S NOT EASY BEING MEAN
SEALED WITH A DISS
BRATFEST AT TIFFANY'S

THE CLIQUE SUMMER COLLECTION:
MASSIE
DYLAN
ALICIA
KRISTEN
CLAIRE (coming August 5)

If you like THE CLIQUE, you may also enjoy:

Bass Ackwards and Belly Up by Elizabeth Craft and Sarah Fain
The **Secrets of My Hollywood Life** series by Jen Calonita
Haters by Alisa Valdes-Rodriguez
Betwixt by Tara Bray Smith
The **Poseur** series by Rachel Maude

For Frankie Boy

In the musty basement of Octavian Country Day School, Skye Hamilton, the eighth-grade alpha, lifted her arms ta-da style.

"So? Whaddaya think?" A tinny clang echoed off the dark walls as an avalanche of gold bangles tumbled down her thin arms. "Is it everything you ever dreamed of, or is it everything you ever dreamed of?"

Massie Block was speechless.

The last time she'd felt *this* shocked was in the fourth grade. She was innocently flipping through *CosmoGIRL!*, passing time while Jakkob painted caramel-colored highlights in her glossy brown hair, when she discovered that bikini waxes were *not* tacky bathing suit–shaped candles. From that day forward, Massie had devoured every magazine, every month, so she would never be that embarrassingly clueless again. But nothing could have ever prepared her for what she and her best friends were staring at now. Not even *Vogue*.

"Do you luh-v the room or do you luh-v the room?" asked a bubbly blonde with Swiss Miss braids—one of Skye's four BFFs, known collectively as the DSL Daters because they made super-fast connections with boys.

"Um." Massie side-glanced at the Pretty Committee, who were staring into the secret room they'd just competed for and won. Their eyes were wide and their mouths hung like Elsa Peretti Open Heart drop earrings.

Kristen Gregory snapped the pink-and-orange terry Puma sweatband around her wrist. Alicia Rivera folded her arms across the black Nanette Lepore shrug that stretched tautly across her C-cups. Dylan Marvil twirled her curly long red hair. And Claire Lyons swiped the white-blond bangs away from her blue eyes.

They had spent weeks fantasizing about this mysterious room and all of the things they would do with it once it was theirs. Secret rendezvous with the Briarwood boys, spa treatments during lunch, an eavesdropper-free place to gossip, a spot to stash spare clothes and makeup. Connie from the Ralph Lauren store was on hold to decorate, and Yuki-San from Zutto was set to deliver sushi on Fridays. But none of that would happen now. Because their private, ultra-luxe eighth-grade retreat had turned out to be a dark cave lit by a single red lightbulb. It smelled like wet toilet paper and dirty fish tank.

Clenching her fists, Massie dug her French-manicured nails into her palms. The sharp stab was painless compared to the rush of humiliation that revved her heart like a massive swig of Red Bull.

How *dare* Skye trick her like that! She'd promised them paradise! This so-called secret campus clubhouse was supposed to give them *status* during their final year at OCD, not night terrors.

Everything blurred. Suddenly, Skye and the four DSL Daters, with their golden hair and matching light gray leggings, looked like a smeared painting of yellow balloons. If word got around OCD that Massie Block had fallen for Skye's stupid practical joke, she'd be done. D-E-A-D, done!

"Skye, you made us compete *Real World/Road Rules Challenge* style for an entire week to find the key to *this*? Gawd! Alicia's dad is so gonna sue you for fraud and mental anguish!" Massie wanted to shout. But that would mean losing control in public. And *that* would mean *lame*.

Instead, she flicked the brim on her olive-green army cap, cocked her chin, and applied a fresh coat of Glossip Girl Original Bubble Gum–flavored lip gloss.

The sweet sugary smell calmed her instantly and gave her the courage she needed to attack. She cleared her throat and the Pretty Committee instantly backed up, taking cover in the dank darkness of the school's basement corridor. They obviously sensed Massie was about to pounce and wanted to give her enough space.

"Skye, are you a Diesel turtleneck poncho?"

Alicia giggled in anticipation. Kristen slapped a hand over her mouth.

"No." Skye, who was casually stretching her hamstrings beside the open door, lowered her leg. The DSL Daters gathered behind the alpha and exchanged a round of what-is-she-tawking-about glances.

Massie took a confident half-step closer to the eighth-graders.

"Then why are you trying to pull one over on me?"

The Pretty Committee burst into hysterical laughter and high-fived Massie. She slapped them back with pride, not caring one bit if they were disrespecting Skye. After all, Skye had disrespected her first by making them compete for a fake room. And what self-respecting alpha would just roll over and take *that*? The days of kissing Skye's Lycra-covered butt were more over than Nick and Jessica.

Pushing back the sleeves of her fuzzy pink angora sweater, Skye wore an expression that was oddly peaceful for an alpha who had just been mocked by a group of seventh-graders. Her robin's-egg-blue eyes looked friendly. Her pillowy lips parted slightly, as though she were too relaxed to even smile.

"Maybe if you had the guts to go inside you wouldn't feel that way."

"Yeah, go in," urged the DSL Dater with the pig nose and long blond ponytail.

"Yeah," echoed the others. "Go on."

Someone tried to shove Massie forward, but she planted the heels of her mocha suede Miu Miu clogs on the graying linoleum and stood firm. Claire stood on her tiptoes and peeked through the narrow space between Dylan's and Alicia's heads.

"What *is* this place?" she whimpered, looking into the dark, musty-smelling room.

"It's OCD's bomb shelter," Skye announced with the enthusiasm of a Disney World tour guide. "It's in the basement, and then even lower. Two stories below Principal Burns's office. Isn't it better than the best?"

"Opposite of yes." Alicia tossed her thick mascara-black hair. "I'd rather get blown up."

"Take a look inside," Skye insisted.

The Pretty Committee instantly huddled together a few feet back from the door. Alicia reached for Massie, who shook her off, refusing to give Skye the satisfaction of knowing she was utterly creeped out.

"Does anyone have a flashlight?" Alicia whispered. "I think I saw the floor move."

"What? Lemme see." Dylan extended her neck. "Ehmagawd! That's not the floor moving—it's snakes!" She hid her face in Kristen's post–soccer game armpit.

"Shut up!" Alicia squeezed past Claire, hiding behind the snickering DSL Daters.

Dylan stuffed her hands in the deep side pockets of her stylishly baggy Earnest Sewn denim overalls. "I think I just heard a tiger."

"Same," agreed the others.

The DSL Daters giggled.

"It's so pathetic." Skye sighed.

Sensing the beginning of a challenge, Massie stiffened. "What is?"

"So many girls fought to win this room. And now you don't even want it." Skye finger-combed her buttery blond waves. "Your fickleness makes me think of those haters who buy pet bunnies and then abandon them when they realize that their pweshious widdle wabbits are wild animals that chew leather flats and leave poo pellets all over their beds."

5

Massie felt as though a Marc Jacobs wedge-heel boot had stomped down on her Pilates-toned abs. "Are you comparing me to an animal abandoner?"

Skye shrugged.

Massie gasped.

"Puh-lease! I so boycotted Burberry when they started using fur."

"It's true." Kristen stepped forward. "She did."

"Yeah!" Dylan cracked her knuckles. "Who do you think made all the WHEN PLAID GOES BAD signs around school?"

"Allie-Rose Singer," blurted Skye as she straightened up from a demi-plié.

"True," Alicia admitted. "But guess who forced her to make them?"

Massie grinned triumphantly.

"Well, if you really loved all creatures as much as I do, you wouldn't be afraid of a few snakes and you'd go in that room."

The prickly sting of adrenaline spread through Massie's entire body. A challenge had been declared. Without a second thought, she reached for Alicia's wrist. Alicia grabbed Kristen's. Kristen grabbed Claire's. And Claire grabbed Dylan's. Like a group of first-graders crossing a busy intersection, the Pretty Committee held hands as Massie dragged them into the glowing red room with its low black ceilings and bone-chilling dampness.

The door slammed shut behind them.

"Ahhhhhh!" As if caught in a swarm of bees, Massie, Kristen, Dylan, and Claire hand-fanned the air with spastic urgency.

"Call 911!" Alicia shrieked.

"What's the number?" Dylan screamed back.

"Ahhhhhh!" Massie ran straight into a sticky spiderweb that stretched all the way from the black stucco ceiling to the snake-covered floor. She batted it off her head but couldn't escape its menacing tickle. It was on her cheek, her arms, and her neck.

Whooooohooooohooooo. Stayyyy outtt offf myyyy rooooommm.

"Ehmagawd, a ghost!" Kristen shouted.

Claire buried her face inside her Forever 21 kelly-green sweater coat.

"Get out of my roooooooooom. GET OUT OF MY ROOOOOOM!" the ghost moaned again.

"Ahhhhhhhh!" The girls raced to the door and pounded and kicked and scratched. "Let! Us! Out!"

All of a sudden, what felt like clumps of slithery, slimy insects dropped from the ceiling, landing in the girls' deep-conditioned hair, on their shoulders and the tips of their designer shoes.

"Ahhhhhh!"

"Scorpions!" Dylan bear-hugged Massie.

"Roaches!" Kristen frantically mussed her sweaty blond hair.

"Locusts!" Claire covered her eyes and jogged in place.

"Ewwww!" Alicia ran in tight circles.

Massie's lifelong credo—to remain cool under any and all circumstances—no longer applied. Snakes, spiderwebs, ghost moans, red bulbs, and tiger snarls made "cool" a nonoption.

"Let us out of here," she panic-begged. "Claire can't breathe!"

"What?" Claire palmed the black walls in search of the exit.

"Re-laxxx!" cackled Skye as she yanked open the heavy black door.

She flipped a switch by the floor, and suddenly the room was flooded with warm golden light. The ceilings were low and the walls were a rich pearly black infused with winking glitter. A mirrored disco ball began spinning above their heads, casting shimmering squares across the hot-dog-shaped room.

"Rubber!" Kristen kicked a heap of black and snot-green toy snakes across the room with her Adidas soccer cleats. "They're rubber."

"*Told* you they weren't real." Massie put a reassuring hand on Claire's shoulder.

Claire giggled with a mix of astonishment and relief.

Skye switched off the iPod docked on a white Bose speaker cube at the back of the room, putting an end to the tiger roars and ghost moans. She clapped twice. "Let's clear this place out and show them what they really won."

Massie stood fixed and firm in the center of the room, suffering from a full-body brain freeze. As the DSL Daters, armed with big green Heftys, whirled about, scooping up handfuls of fake reptiles and insects, she tried to formulate a fitting comeback or ultra-cool reaction. Something that would help her regain the pride she'd lost while banging on the dark walls, begging for mercy. Something that would show the DSL Daters they'd messed with the wrong girls. Something that might convince them the Pretty Committee had known it was a joke all along. But nothing came to mind.

All Massie could think about was how angry she was at Skye for humiliating her in front of so many alphas. And how, in a weird sort of way, she was impressed by the intricacy of the joke. Maybe even *inspired*. Sort of like in those rare moments at school when someone showed up in a better outfit than hers. After the jealousy wore off, Massie always found herself reenergized and ready to do better. Of course, *this* was a zillion times more extreme than a case of outfit envy, but the desire to become a better alpha was the same. And for that, she was grateful and ready to move on.

"I'm flattered." Massie finger-tossed her bangs.

The Pretty Committee's perfectly waxed brows knit together in confusion, probably wondering where she could have possibly been taking this.

"Flattered?" Skye sounded slightly disappointed by Massie's sudden composure. *Perfect.*

"Yeah." Massie helped herself to one of the five pink faux-fur-covered director's chairs that faced a Samsung flat-screen mounted on the far wall. "You ah-bviously put a lot of effort into this. Which means you wanted to impress us. So thanks." She wiggled her butt toward the back of the fluffy seat and reclined. "I wish *we* had that much free time. But we're always sooo busy, right, girls?"

"Right," the Pretty Committee answered back with over-the-top enthusiasm as they filled the empty pink chairs beside Massie.

"It didn't take us *that* long, did it?" Skye turned to the other DSL Daters for backup, but they were too occupied with their cleanup job to notice.

"Whatevs." Massie glanced around the dank, empty space, making it clear that she was unimpressed. "So where's the *real* room?"

"Here." Skye beamed, splaying her arms like a flight attendant indicating a plane's exits.

The DSL Daters put down their trash bags and rallied beside Skye, under the silver monitor, their blond heads lining up with the bottom of the screen like a row of sunflowers.

"This is *it*?" Alicia's MAC Lipglass–covered top lip rose in disgust.

Skye and the DSL Daters nodded with delight.

"It's a long sausage with five chairs and a TV," Kristen snapped.

"A burnt black sausage," Dylan insisted.

Claire giggled.

"Too funny! They think this is an *ordinary* TV," Skye said to the DSL Daters, who snickered at the thought.

"This *tee-veeee* just so happens to be the best-kept secret in the country." Skye pulled a remote covered in pink Swarovski crystals out from under her rose-colored bra strap. "Maybe even the world." She pressed a button and the screen hummed to life.

"We had a pink shag throw rug, five electronic foot spas, a movie-theater popcorn maker, a real Starbucks latte machine, two racks of spare clothes, and a makeup vanity fully stocked with the complete line of Hard Candy cosmetics in here, but we moved them out for the prank," offered the DSL dater with long blond braids. "Everything will be back next—"

"Move!" Skye hissed. Swiss Miss Braids hurried to the left of the screen and stood behind her. "It's on."

A black-and-white image appeared on the screen. It was a shot of an empty classroom. The picture was gritty but still clear enough that it could be deciphered. There were no desks, only plastic cafeteria chairs arranged in a semicircle. Behind them were posters of wide sunbeams searing through fluffy clouds; a single drop of rain in an otherwise still puddle; football players in a postgame huddle, hugging. Beside each image was a stanza of poetry written in white, swirling script that was too far away to read.

Massie side-glanced at the Pretty Committee, wondering if they had any idea what was so great about a low-def image of an empty classroom, in black and white, no less.

"Um, Skye . . ." Massie snickered. "Dylan doesn't get it."

Dylan smacked Massie's dark-denim-encased thigh.

"Have you ever wondered what boys are thinking?" Skye waved the pink crystal-covered remote. "I mean, *really* thinking?"

Everyone nodded slowly, even the DSL Daters.

Skye clasped her hands behind her back and began pacing beneath the screen. "Sure, they say they like you, but then they never text. Or they invite you to a dance and then hang out with their stupid friends all night. And how about acting like they don't know you in public even if you spent the entire night before IM'ing? Don't *even* try to ask if something's wrong. All they'll do is shrug and grunt and punch their buddies."

"Too true!" the DSL Daters hollered back.

Massie shifted uncomfortably, crossing one leg, then the next. Skye's little rant was way too on-target. At boy/girl parties, her crush, Derrington, always spent more time with Cam Fisher, Kemp Hurley, Josh Hotz, and Chris Plovert than with her. And he responded to texts with one-word answers. In fact, just last week Massie IM'd him with the latest on Melly Kantor's post-yoga B.O. And how did he respond?

With an *F*.

A lone *F* for *funny*. Not even a *TF* for *too funny*.

Just a single *F*.

All weekend long, Massie wondered if Derrington was turned off because she'd mentioned B.O., or if he was somehow related to Melly and offended by the incriminating gossip. More than anything, she wanted to run these possibilities by the Pretty Committee for analysis. But she didn't want them to think she was insecure about boys. So she suffered in silence.

"I never have boyfriend angst." Massie sighed, crossing her fingers.

The Pretty Committee shook their heads, signaling that they didn't either.

"That's because you don't have *boyfriends*," snickered Swiss Miss Braids.

"Opposite of true!" Alicia snapped.

Massie opened her mouth, ready to second that, but Skye didn't give her a chance.

"You may be too young for a serious relationship, but you're never too young to know what boys are thinking. Because once you know *that,* you'll know how to get whatever you want and *whom*ever you want."

The DSL Daters giggle-agreed.

"Ehmagawd, that totally explains it!" Dylan blurted.

"'Splains what?" Skye nibbled on her pillowy bottom lip and tilted her head. A mass of perfectly conditioned blond waves swung alongside her jaw.

"How you always get the A-list hawties."

Skye stopped pacing and stared deep into Dylan's green eyes. "Um, we're not exactly ugly."

Dylan's cheeks reddened. "I didn't mean it like *that.*"

"She meant more like how you're so confident around boys and how you always know the right things to say," Kristen chimed in.

Skye affectionately tapped the TV screen.

The Pretty Committee leaned closer while Massie's brain flooded with possibilities, all of which led to her becoming a world-renowned guy expert. She would own a fleet of purple Lexus convertibles with license plates that read BOYS R US.

"Wait." Her brain suddenly snapped back to reality. "How is a room filled with tacky posters from Spencer's Gifts gonna teach you about boys?"

"Is this screen kinda like a crystal ball?" Claire made Massie-esque air quotes when she said "crystal ball."

"Better." Skye grinned.

"How can it be *better*?" Alicia squinted suspiciously.

"Because *this* classroom is where the Briarwood Boys have ESP," Skye whisper-announced.

"Huh?" asked Alicia.

"Emotional Sensitivity Powwows," the DSL Daters said at the same time.

"You mean all that Dr. Loni stuff?" Dylan asked, half-jokingly referring to the famous radio PhD who taught "emotionally illiterate men" (and convicts) how to "tune into their thoughts" and "translate them into feelings."

"Yup." Skye nodded. "He's their teacher. He's been doing it on the DL for five years."

The Pretty Committee gasped.

"Ehmagawd! My mom has been trying to get him on *The Daily Grind* forever." Dylan pulled her mint-green LG Chocolate phone out of her back pocket. "But he won't do women's talk shows, only men's." She pulled out her phone and began to speed-dial. "Merri-Lee Marvil is nawt going to believe this."

"Drop it!" grunted Swiss Miss Braids right before she slapped Dylan's phone away from her ear.

Dylan fumbled to catch it.

"You can't tell a soul."

"Shhhh." Skye lifted a pink-manicured finger to her lips, causing another bracelet avalanche. "The boys agreed to take the class if, and only if, it was kept under wraps. If they ever knew we had a camera in there we'd be . . ."

She slid her index finger across the center of her long neck, then dangled her tongue from the corner of her mouth, like a thirsty cat.

Massie could hardly sit still. She was being handed a gift that, until now, she'd assumed only gawd had. The ability to know what boys were thinking would guarantee that she'd always say the right thing—no more awkward silent periods when flirting! The fear of getting dumped would be gone, because the Pretty Committee would know all pre-dump signs, so they could do it first. They would never be heartbroken or embarrassed or insecure again. But most of all, Massie Block would finally become the all-knowing boy expert she had always wanted to be, running clinics and seminars on topics like "Understanding Boys," "Outfits Guys Will Love," and "Why Asking 'What's Wrong?' *Is* What's Wrong." Everyone would turn to her for the answers, and for the first time ever, she would have them.

"Where's the camera hidden?" asked Kristen.

"In the Share Bear." Skye rolled her blue eyes, as if it should have been obvious.

Claire giggled. "My screen name is ClaireBear."

"ClaireBear," Dylan burped.

Kristen and Alicia burst out laughing.

"Enough," Massie snapped, mostly to show Skye she had a tight rein on the Pretty Committee.

They stopped laughing and Skye shot Massie a thank-you nod before continuing. Massie nodded back, relishing the invisible alpha respect waves that flowed between them.

"The Share Bear is a blue-and-white stuffed animal. The guys can only speak if Dr. Loni gives it to them. It's his *thing*."

The girls leaned forward in their fuzzy pink chairs, anxious to hear more.

"Who put the camera in it?" Claire asking, sounding mesmerized.

Skye shrugged. "All I know is that it's there, and that you'll never have to wonder who likes who, why, and for how long again. It's the best when you're trying to pick a suitable date for a dance or something. Not that you're ready for those things yet."

The DSL Daters snickered.

Massie's heart quickened. "What's that supposed to mean?"

"It's just that the only time we see you with boys is at the soccer games. And even then, you're more into talking to each other than to them."

Massie's cheeks burned with rage and humiliation. Was Skye right? Did everyone at OCD think they were guy-shy? Her mother's *Cosmopolitan* magazines always told women to act aloof and play hard-to-get. So that's how she advised the Pretty Committee. But what if their advice was *wrong*? Was aloof *out*? Had she been reading old issues by accident? Or was the whole *Cosmo* thing just an excuse to avoid embarrassing herself in public? The questions came faster than the answers. All Massie knew for sure was that the Pretty Committee would have to put on a show worthy of the Pussycat Dolls at the next dance.

Skye placed her palm on the black-glitter-infused walls, turned to the side, and pliéd. "Maybe when you get to the eighth grade that will change and you'll start to *really* discover guys and—"

"Wait!" Claire interrupted. "I *have* a boyfriend."

"Same!" Massie insisted.

"I'm close," Alicia lied.

"Anyone else?" Skye scanned the row of fuzzy pink director's chairs.

Kristen lowered her head, focusing on an imaginary piece of dirt under her perfectly filed pinky nail, and Dylan tugged at her eyelashes as if trying to remove an annoying mascara clump.

"I thought so," Skye boasted, pointing her left leg front, side, then back. "Anyway, I'm hosting an end-of-year costume party, and the theme is famous couples. Since you're next in line for the room, you get an automatic invite."

The Pretty Committee silent-clapped, knowing what an honor this was, while Massie tried to think of the fastest way to spread the news around school. An informative e-mail "accidentally" sent to the wrong person? A casual mention in a crowded bathroom? A detailed note dropped in the middle of an assembly?

"But you all need dates," Skye warned. "*Suitable* ones. No B-listers," she said, pronouncing the term "blisters."

"Or they can go as the Cheetah Girls," Ponytail scoffed, and then exchanged a high five with Swiss Miss Braids.

"We *have* boyfriends," Dylan shouted above their laughter.

"And even if we broke up with them, we could always find newer, more *suitable* ones like *that*," Alicia snapped. "Thanks to ESP."

The Pretty Committee squealed with delight.

"Um, reminder." Skye stepped in from of the screen. "This room isn't yours until next year. Alicia, Dylan, and Kristen will have to find boyfriends all by themselves."

"And if we can't?" Kristen twisted the pink-and-orange terry Puma sweatband around her wrist.

"If you *can't* . . ." Skye wound her thick blond waves into a high ballerina bun and fastened it with one of her gold bangles. "You cute, itty-bitty little seventh-graders will be forced to walk around my party sucking these." She held out her hand and Thin-Pin, the DSL Dater with ultra-fine straight blond hair, slapped five pink pacifiers in her palm.

Alicia, Dylan, and Kristen gasped.

Massie and Claire exchanged "phew" glances, knowing that their pre-established relationships with Cam and Derrington rendered them automatically immune to the humiliating ultimatum.

"FYI . . ." Skye slid the pacifiers onto her fingers, held out her arm, cocked her head, and admired them. "If one of you fails, you all fail."

"Wait!" Massie heard herself protest aloud. "That's not fair."

The Pretty Committee gasped again in a thanks-a-lot sort of way.

"I mean . . ." Massie giggle-blushed. "This whole *thing* isn't fair. Everyone will ah-bviously *try* to get dates but if for some reason someone falls through at the last minute, you can't punish all of—"

"Do you *all* want access to this room next year?"

They nodded.

"Then you will *all* be treated the same."

"That's how it works," announced Swiss Miss Braids.

"We had the same rules when we were in the seventh grade," said Ponytail.

The other blondes nodded in agreement.

"No problem." Massie grinned. "If we got Birkin bags before Mary-Kate and Ashley, we can certainly find a couple of boyfriends."

"I like your confidence." Skye smiled, flashing a row of iPod-white, never-needed-braces teeth.

Massie half-nodded in thanks.

"I just hope you're right, or your lives are going to *suck*." Skye wiggled her pacifier fingers again, and the DSL Daters cracked up.

Instantly, the Pretty Committee turned toward Massie, anxious for her to unleash a paralyzing comeback.

But it was best to hold back. If Skye knew they were worried, it would only increase her alpha power and weaken Massie's own. Instead, she inhaled, yoga style, focusing on the sharpness of her breath until the sensation calmed her. Finally, she managed a cool smile. "Not a problem—we have more options than Match.com."

"I hope so, because the party's only three weeks away."

Skye clapped once, letting everyone know it was time to leave. She pressed her thumb into the remote and flicked off the lights.

And just like *that*, the Pretty Committee's excitement faded with the image of the TV screen.

CURRENT STATE OF THE UNION	
IN	**OUT**
GBS (Gossiping in Bomb Shelters)	GBS (Gossiping in Bathroom Stalls)
ESP	IM
Sucker practice	Soccer practice

Outside Slice of Heaven—a windowless brick igloo designed to look like a giant pizza oven—the Pretty Committee re-glossed and finger-combed while Massie twirled her low side-pony and examined their outfits for embarrassing latte stains and outdated accessories.

As she stood in a cluster to the right of the door, Claire couldn't help wondering if the other girls knew they were going to see the boys after school, because their outfits were all 8.5s or higher, and her ensemble—a faded camo long-sleeved waffle shirt, cuffed khaki cargos, and olive-green Keds slip-ons—made her look like a jalapeño pepper.

"Does this kimono dress make me look too wide?" Dylan smoothed the red-and-white satin over her black leggings as if trying to stretch it.

Massie lowered her oversize Chloé sunglasses, peering over the tops of the purple lenses.

"No. Your broad shoulders balance your hips."

Dylan grinned and then stuck a loose red curl back in her messy updo.

"Are my Seven cutoffs too last year?" Kristen stuffed her hands into the pockets of the denim blazer she wore over one of Alicia's old white cashmere hoodies.

21

Massie tapped her chin. "No. You updated them with navy leggings. But good question."

"Phew." Kristen wiped imaginary sweat from her forehead.

"Does my lavender Splendid look snowboarderish under this white short-sleeved blouse?" Alicia wondered.

"That's nawt just a blouse," Massie corrected. "It's a Daryl K. And Daryl K can never look snowboarderish. It's too high style."

"Point." Alicia beamed.

"Now me." Massie spun, modeling her gray fitted short-sleeved blazer, long turquoise satin cami, and dark DKNY jeans, which were tucked into flat black riding boots. "Do I look *too* cute, or just cute enough?"

"Too cute," they all answered at once.

"Perf!" Massie clapped silently.

"Now, remember . . . ." Kristen wrapped a pale hand around the shellacked-dinner-roll door handle outside the restaurant. "Act surprised when you see the guys. If they know we followed them after practice, they'll call us 'soccer-stalkers' for, like, the next ten years."

Claire's insides leapt. Cam Fisher was on the other side of the door. There was nothing better than running into her crush on a school night. It was an unexpected treat, like finding five dollars in an old pair of jeans or getting a last-minute dinner at McDonald's—only better. She cursed herself one last time for looking like a jalapeño and then pushed her insecurities aside. After all, wasn't love supposed to be blind?

"One more thing." Massie swatted Kristen's hand off the

hard, glistening dinner roll and pulled the girls aside into a last-minute huddle. "We're here to find boyfriends." She half-smiled at Claire. "I mean, *they* are here to find boyfriends. Kuh-laire and I already have them."

Claire full-smiled back, unable to hide her joy. For once, she had more in common with Massie than the others. And it was nice to be on the enviable side of things.

"Wait until everyone hears we showed up at Skye Hamilton's eighth-grade graduation party with hawt, suitable guys," Alicia said to her reflection in Massie's tinted Chloés. "Our alpha status will be a given until college at least."

"Calvin Klein will name a perfume after us called Envy," Dylan announced.

"Gucci already has a perfume called Envy," Kristen noted.

"Well, then Calvin's will be called Envy *Us*."

"Point." Alicia high-fived her.

"And if you don't find dates, it'll be called Sucks 2 B Us," Massie reminded them.

"Point." Alicia stuffed her high-five hand into the back pocket of her stretch J Brand jeans.

"Kuh-laire, it's up to you to show the others how to flirt." Massie pinched her cheeks rosy.

"No problem," Claire assured her, while having no clue how to pull this off.

Massie stepped aside to let pass a pregnant woman in a light blue T-shirt that said IT'S NOT EASY BEING EASY across the belly. "Since it's going to be an eighth-grade party, your dates should be mature and cool."

"You mean like *Derrington*?" Kristen snickered.

"What's *that* supposed to mean?"

"Nothing." Kristen's cheeks reddened.

"Tell me."

"Nothing."

"Tell!" Massie insisted.

"It's just that Derrington wiggles his butt when he's happy, and he wears shorts in the winter."

"So?"

"So . . ." Kristen looked to the others for backup but they lowered their heads. "Is that *mature*?"

"No!" Massie threw open the door like she meant it. "It's ah-dorable!" She marched inside the domed restaurant, which smelled like warm dough and tangy oregano.

Slice of Heaven was the Starbucks of pizza. "Slice Stylists" offered everything from soy crusts to lactose-free cheese, and sauce infusions that promised zit-free skin (pomegranate seeds), higher grades (ginkgo biloba), and weight loss (Hoodia extract). Bright orange flames flickered on the white brick walls, making diners feel like they were inside a massive pizza oven.

"How come we never eat here?" Claire asked, searching the crowded restaurant for Cam.

"If I wanted to fry, I'd go to St. Barts." Massie fanned her face, the faux fire reflecting in her eyes.

"Point." Alicia wiggled beside Massie, shoving Claire into a tower made of ceramic takeout boxes, aka the hostess stand.

"Welcome to Slice of Heaven. How many in your party?" asked a willowy blond college-age girl wearing a white tank dress and a headband with a bobbing silvery halo.

"Five," Dylan announced. "Can you please put us near some ma-tour boys?"

"Um." The girl tapped the menus against her pointy Reese Witherspoon chin while scanning the pie-shaped tables. "Right now everything is taken."

"How 'bout back there." Massie pointed. "By those guys in the soccer uniforms."

"There aren't any available—"

"Thanks, Angel." Massie grabbed the round menus from the hostess's hand. "We can seat ourselves."

The hostess called after the Pretty Committee, but they snaked through the tables, giggling all the way to the back of the restaurant.

The space behind Claire's belly button tingled with nervous excitement as they approached a pack of fifteen boys in burgundy shorts and green shirts. They were seated elbow-to-elbow around four circular tables that had been jammed together, their two coaches keeping a watchful eye from a nearby booth. The whole team seemed to be there—everyone except Cam.

Claire felt a sudden twinge of disappointment in the very place her nervous excitement had just been.

"Ehmagawd, what are you guys doing here?" Kristen shouted, much louder than she needed to. "Look, it's the Briarwood Tomahawks. I swear, this is so freaky, isn't it?"

"Wow, I don't believe it!" Alicia pressed a hand against her white blouse as though the shock might trigger heart failure.

"Block!" Derrington shouted while jamming a piece of what looked like chocolate-covered pizza in his mouth. Comb tracks through his usually messy blond hair confirmed a post-practice shower.

"Oh, hey there." Massie raised her waxed brows just high enough to make her surprise seem genuine. Then she turned back to the PC. "Don't forget the mission. Suitable dates. No blisters. HART guys only," she reminded them before making her way over to the head of the table where her star goalie of a crush was seated.

"What's HART?" whispered Claire.

"Hawt, Alpha, Rich, and Toned," Alicia explained.

"Oh."

"Ready?" asked Massie, turning toward to the head of the table where Derrington was sitting, wearing a red-and-white-checked napkin as a bib.

They nodded in recognition, then parted ways.

"What are the odds?" Dylan reached over one of Kemp Hurley's well-defined shoulders and lifted a limp bacon-wrapped mozzarella stick out of a gold metal basket.

"This sugar bun's a hungry one," Kemp, the team's biggest perv, said with a devilish smile.

"Dy-*lan*," Alicia whisper-hissed. "Put it back."

"Why?" Dylan lowered the mozzarella stick to the table and swished it around the bowl of ranch dressing.

"Put. It. Back." Alicia muttered through the side of her mouth. "Chris Plovert is *staring* at you."

"Oh! Sorry." Dylan blushed. "Were you about to eat this?"

The perma-tanned brunet shook his head no, then burped. "It's all you."

Dylan immediately swallowed a mouthful of air and burped back, "Thanks."

Plovert's mouth hung open in disbelief.

"See," Dylan smirked and then devoured the stick in a single bite. "No one was eating it."

"It's not *that*." Alicia rolled her eyes.

"What then?"

"Kuh-laire, will *you* tell her?"

"Tell her *what?*" Claire knew she sounded impatient, but she was too busy trying to figure out where Cam might be to care.

"That she's never going to *find* a boy if she *acts* like a boy. A girl shouldn't eat in front of her crush until they're married. It's a turn-awff," Alicia explained.

"Oh." Claire immediately thought of the bags of gummy worms and sours that Cam had given her over the last nine months and wondered if she'd been wrong to devour them on the spot.

"That's so stupid." Dylan grabbed a half-eaten crust off Kemp's plate and stuffed it in her mouth. "Are you guys turned off by me?" she asked, sticking out her A-cups ever so slightly.

"*Au contraire,* honey bear." Kemp winked. Chris shook his

head and lifted his frothy chocolate milk shake to his wide mouth.

"Do *you* want to tell Massie you're blowing the mission, or should *we*?" Alicia grabbed Kristen's thin wrist and pulled her to the other side of the table.

"No, wait!" Dylan followed them to the head of the table.

Suddenly, Claire was alone. She didn't know if she should follow her friends (follower?), make small talk with the boys (cheating on Cam?), or leave (pathetic!). All she knew for sure was that lurking solo behind the Tomahawks' table made her a shoo-in for the title of Soccer-Stalker.

"Hey, you," beckoned a sweet male voice behind her. The familiar citrus-meets-oak smell of Drakkar Noir practically lifted Claire out of her olive-green Keds.

"Hey!" She turned, then blushed at the sight of Cam's gorgeous blue eye and green eye. She wanted to hug him just for being there. So she did.

From across the table, Massie gave her an approving thumbs-up, then nudged the others to make sure they'd follow Claire's flirty example.

Cam took her hand and led her to his seat beside Derrington.

"Hey, Fisher." Massie playfully smacked his firm bicep. "Nice of you to finally show up."

Cam sat down and pulled Claire onto his lap. "I was in the bathroom."

"*Pffffffft.*" Derrington offered up his best mouth-fart.

"*Mature,*" Kristen mouthed to Massie, who rolled her

eyes in a you-don't-know-what-you're-talking-about sort of way.

"Shut up, toilet-clogger!" Cam punched the side of his arm.

"That was Plovert, not me!" Derrington reddened.

"Was not!" Plovert shouted as he whipped a greasy slice of pepperoni at Derrington's cheek.

"Was too," Cam insisted. "And by 'too,' I mean numba two!"

Dylan cracked up and then added a *"perrrrrrp."*

Cam swiveled in his seat and lifted his palm to high-five her.

"Grow up, Dylan," Alicia snapped, loud enough for her Polo-loving semi-crush Josh Hotz to hear from the far end of the table. His chocolate-brown eyes were hidden under a navy-blue New York Yankees cap, but he seemed to be looking their way. "People are trying to eat!"

"How would *you* know about eating?" Dylan snapped.

"From watching *you*!"

"This is a disaster," Massie whispered in Claire's ear. "Flirt again."

"How?" Claire mouthed.

Massie shrugged and glared, in an I-don't-know-but-think-of-something-fast sort of way.

Claire pulled Cam's heavy black JanSport backpack off the ground and heaved it onto her lap. She'd always wondered what he stuffed in there, and now was as good a time as any to find out.

"What are you doing?" Cam shifted his weight, rocking Claire from side to side, until he settled.

"Looking for fun things to play with." She unzipped the main pouch in a single semicircular motion.

Massie air-clapped and nudged the others again, hoping this time they might pay closer attention.

"Forget it." Cam reached around her waist and gripped the bag.

"Why?" Claire giggle-swatted his hands away.

"It's not polite," he said in a fake girly voice. "You might find my tampons."

"Ew!" Alicia rolled her eyes in disgust.

Claire hated that Cam knew what tampons were. What if he thought she actually used them? The notion filled her with so much nervous energy, she thrust her hand inside his backpack and accidentally smashed her knuckle into the spine of a notebook. The pain was sobering. "Are you hiding presents for me?" She managed to ask despite the throbbing.

Massie shot her a quick thumbs-up, silently encouraging Claire to press on.

"Yes!" Cam giggle-tugged the bag away.

"Liar!" She giggle-tugged it back.

"I swear!"

"We'll see about that!"

With a final tug Claire managed to recapture the bag. "See ya!" She stuffed it under her arm like a football and serpentined around the tables as if charging the end zone.

"You're dead, Lyons!" Cam shouted as he chased after her. "Give it back!"

Dylan, Alicia, Kristen, and Massie began chanting Claire's name, encouraging her to run faster and go, go, go. Which she did, all the way to the very last stall in the ladies' bathroom, where she caught her breath and wondered what Cam could possibly be hiding.

The restaurant's doughy aroma was replaced by that of the pineapple-scented hand soap or tile cleaner or whatever it was that made the all-white bathroom smell like Hawaiian Tropic.

Claire lowered the wooden lid of the toilet seat and sat down. She placed the backpack on her lap and peered inside. The scent of pencil erasers and fermented red apples shot out like an invisible geyser.

It was funny how something as simple as having Cam's knapsack made her feel closer to him. Like he was there with her and they were connected and—

"Claire, give it back!" he shouted as he banged on the door.

"Go away, young man!" she bleated in her best old-lady voice.

Part of her felt ashamed for being so obvious and flirty with Cam. And part of her couldn't wait to see what he was hiding. A love poem? A bag of gummy bears? A burned CD of songs that made him think of her?

She reached inside and pulled out a black-and-white composition notebook. Anxious to catch a glimpse of his handwriting and to see the kind of notes he took (detailed vs. single word, possible margin doodles of her?), Claire opened it. All three postcards she had sent him from L.A.—of the Santa Monica Pier, Grauman's Chinese Theatre, the Hollywood sign—fell to the oatmeal-colored floor. Her heart filled and floated like a hot air balloon. *He'd kept them!*

"No snooping!" Cam shouted, as if he was watching her.

"I'm *not*." She stuffed the postcards between the pages and then heard a light *ping*.

A thin metal paper clip had fallen out of the notebook and landed on the tile floor. And then a folded piece of paper floated onto her lap. Claire leaned forward to retrieve the paper clip and a flurry of loose papers tumbled out.

Knowing full well she should quickly attach them back in place without peeking, Claire nonetheless felt compelled to at least glance at a page or two. How else would she put them respectfully back in the right order?

Cam banged on the door again, a little harder and a little longer than he had before.

"Claire, give me back my stuff." His voice sounded more serious this time.

"Coming," Claire muttered while "respectfully" scanning what appeared to be a collection of printed IM conversations . . . with someone named Nikki. His messages were typed in Courier while *hers* were in some swirly-girly font that automatically dotted the *i*'s with hearts.

Claire's pulse thumped loudly in her ears. Phrases like "camp this summer" and "when I wore your leather jacket" and "Valentine's Day gift" cut her like a pair of super-sharp cuticle clippers to the heart.

"This isn't funny." Cam's voice cracked. "I thought I could trust you."

"You can." She stuffed the papers in the notebook and shoved it toward the bottom of his bag, wishing all she'd found was a crinkled Ziploc filled with sours.

"Then gimme me back my stuff."

He sounded impatient, if not slightly angry.

Claire zipped up the backpack and hurried toward the exit. Feeling that surge of nervous energy, she leaned with all her weight and smashed into Cam. Normally, the collision would have cracked them up, but she wasn't feeling particularly *normal*. Instead, they quickly separated and glared suspiciously at each other.

Claire dropped the backpack in Cam's open arms. "You're acting like you have something to hide."

"That's because I do."

Her pulse quickened.

"What is it?"

Without a single word, he turned and zigzagged his way around the bustling waiters and returned to his table.

"What are you hiding?" Claire hurried after him, clutching her roiling stomach.

"Your present," he answered.

"Yeah, right," she mumbled.

He sat and turned toward Derrington, trying to feign interest in a joke he was telling Massie about a tuba player and a burrito salesman.

Claire stuck her tongue out at the number 2 on the back

of Cam's green soccer shirt and helped herself to a seat at the empty four-top behind them. She flipped open her red Swarovski-crystal covered cell and pretended to make a call.

Massie immediately left Derrington's side and joined her. The rest of the Pretty Committee followed.

"What happened?" Massie shouted over the blasting stereo, where some angry rock guy was scream-singing about his desperate need for blood. "Are you okay?"

Claire shook her head no.

"I knew it!"

"How did you know?"

"You're faking a phone call so you can have private time to think without looking like an LBR." Massie pointed at the sparkling Motorola in Claire's palm. "I taught you that trick, remember?"

Claire nodded. She wanted to smile, but her face felt too heavy for the task.

"Did you find anything juicy?" Alicia leaned forward in her seat. She slowly gathered her glossy black hair and tossed it to the left side of her neck, showing off her "better side" in case any HARTs were watching.

"Not really."

"Then why aren't you sitting together anymore?" asked Dylan, pulling up a fifth chair.

Claire shrugged, and then side-glanced at Cam, who was side-glancing at her. She quickly looked away.

"Well, *something* must have happened." Alicia put her arm around Claire's shoulders. "I can tell just by looking at—"

"Who's *that*?" Kristen tilted her head toward the busboy one table over. He was hand-sweeping pizza scraps into a gray plastic bin. His jeans were straighter than Alicia's. At first Claire couldn't understand the attraction—and then he turned around. His eyes were army green and as round as the Target logo. Against his zitless clear skin, they resembled the two olives in Mr. Block's après-work martini.

"Done, done, and done. I found my date," Kristin told the PC.

"Ew, the busboy?" Massie's face contorted like she'd bitten into a lemon.

"Yeah, he's kinda hawt," Kristen whispered.

"He's a *busboy*," Massie practically spat.

"He's a total HART." Kristen defended the stranger.

"Minus the R." Massie smirked. "Which makes him a HAT."

Dylan and Alicia giggled.

"So?"

"So?" Alicia held up her palm, letting Massie know she would take it from here. "So don't you think someone in *your* position should be going after someone with a little more—"

"Height?" Kristen asked, sincerely.

"Nooo," Alicia said in guess-again sort of way.

"Body mass?"

Dylan snickered.

"Noooo."

She gazed at her potential crush while he bobbed his head to the angry death rock that roared though the speakers. *"What?"*

"Money!" Massie blurted.

Alicia and Dylan nodded in agreement.

"Huh?"

"Kris, you're always complaining about being p-o-o-r," Massie whisper-spelled. "So maybe you should get attracted to rich guys."

"He ah-bviously has a job."

All of a sudden Derrington plopped himself down on Massie's lap. She shifted uncomfortably.

"You're *poor*?" he asked.

Kristen shot Massie a thanks-a-lot look.

Claire's stomach sympathy-dropped for Kristen and her spilled secret.

"I didn't mean *Kristen's* poor—I meant she has poor taste when it comes to guys," Massie covered.

"There's nothing *poor* about Griffin Hastings," Derrington offered.

"Huh?" Massie squirmed, making zero effort to hide her sudden discomfort. "How do you know him?"

"He's in one of my classes."

Massie's amber eyes widened. "The busboy goes to Briarwood?"

Kristen beamed.

"Yeah, his dad owns, like, twenty theme restaurants on the East Coast. He's being groomed to take over."

"How do you think this song got on the stereo?" Derrington added as he slipped his arm around Massie's neck. "This is practically *his* place."

"Why didn't I know about him?" Alicia asked with a trace of jealousy.

Massie made a fist and stamped the table. "Ah-pproved."

"Yay!" Kristen air-clapped as she watched Griffin wipe the back of a vinyl chair. "Ehmagawd." She gripped Massie's arm. "Is that a book in his back pocket?"

"Beware! He's a huge horror geek," Derrington warned. "Griffin is going to suck your bloooood!" He took a pretend bite out of Massie's neck.

"Ouch!" She pushed him to his feet.

"*What?* I didn't really bite," he pleaded.

"Well, it hurt." Massie rubbed her neck.

"Let me kiss it better."

"Nawt in public," she hissed.

"Whatever!" Derrington stood and stormed back to his table.

"Gawd, he can be so immature!" Massie rolled her eyes.

Claire knew Massie well enough to know she was suddenly looking at Derrington through Skye's eyes, wondering if he had enough HART to impress the alpha, and starting to doubt it.

"Anyway, back to the mission." Massie turned to Kristen. "So? Are you going to ask him?"

"I do love that he reads . . ." Kristen replied.

"Then *ask* him."

"Not yet," Kristen told her. "I have to get to know him a little better."

Claire peeked at Cam again. This time he smiled back. And

Claire couldn't help hoping that maybe Nikki was a young camper with a crush. Perhaps he'd kept the IMs to avoid hurting her feelings, or maybe he'd made them up for a creative writing class or . . .

Suddenly a girl in a pink Splendid hoodie with bobbed brown hair, full high-glossed lips, and gold aviator glasses appeared at their table with an extra-large pizza balancing in the palm of her hand. She wasn't dressed anything like the other Sauce Stylists.

"Here's your pie." She carefully handed it to Massie.

"Um, doubt it." Massie pushed her hand aside.

"Is your name Massie Block?"

"Yeah."

"Then enjoy." She grinned from behind the gold aviators, dropped the pizza on the table, and bolted.

"I'm so nawt eating this." Massie glanced at the boys' table to make sure they'd heard her.

"I'll have it." Dylan reached for a slice, then stopped. "Ehmagawd, *look*."

The Pretty Committee leaned forward, examined the pizza, and gasped. Written in tiny sausage crumbles, it said, SKYE WILL PICK U UP AT 1 P.M. ON SAT. B READY.

Massie slammed the box shut. "Ehmagawd, she's watching us." Her voice quaked as she scanned the crowded, igloo-shaped restaurant. "You guys need to find dates ay-sap or we're gonna have to—"

"You're being paranoid," Kristen insisted.

"Why else would *she* want to see me?"

"Point." Alicia lifted her finger in the air.

"Hurry, pick someone."

"But it's so hard to decide," Dylan whisper-whined. "We don't even know half of these guys. What if we pick Blisters by mistake?"

"Kristen, go ask Griffin," Massie pressed.

"He's a rocker. What if he hates blondes?"

"No one hates blondes," Massie snapped.

"Well, what if he hates soccer?"

"Or scholarships," Dylan added.

"Thanks." Kristen sneered.

A pack of St. Catherine's girls wearing blue-and-white kilts and birthday hats sat at the table behind them. Two mothers stood impatiently while Kristen's crush scrambled to wipe down their table. The girls, on the other hand, were so giddy and happy that Claire wanted to chuck the silver napkin dispenser at their heads.

"If only we could get into the room and hear—" Alicia stopped talking when Massie kicked her shin.

"Shhhh. No one is allowed to know."

"You're so lucky you have Cam." Dylan sighed.

"Yeah, real lucky." Claire sighed back, then lowered her head onto the sticky tabletop.

Claire desperately wanted to tell them about Nikki, but she knew she would have to wait. The day's mission was to *find* boyfriends, not lose them.

One of the coaches signed the check and the boys reached for their jackets.

Cam finally caught Claire's eye long enough to motion for her to come over.

She did. And he pulled her back onto his lap. Only sitting with Cam was different this time, like this new lack of trust between them had created an invisible barrier that kept their bodies from melting together like they had before. Claire no longer felt like she was sinking into a warm beanbag. It was more like sitting on a cold brick. She couldn't help wondering if Cam felt it too, because his arms weren't resting on her lower back like they had been before. In fact, they weren't touching her at all.

"Do you want your present now?" he asked softly.

"You *really* have a present for me?"

He unzipped the outside pocket of his JanSport and pulled out a clear baggie filled with red cinnamon hearts. He swung them in front of her dark blue eyes like a hypnotist's watch. "Of course. That's why I didn't want you to snoop."

"So that's the real reason? The hearts?"

"Yup." Cam dug through the plastic bag, avoiding her eyes. He pulled out a small handful and dropped them into her open mouth.

Claire closed her eyes, fighting the fiery sting of cinnamon. Then she bit down.

They were stale and hard to swallow.

Just like Cam's excuse.

Hooking a freshly manicured finger around the sage Dupioni silk curtains in the front foyer of the Block estate, Massie peered outside. A mild mix of sun and clouds had inspired her to wear her gold-and-silver-striped V-neck Eila Moss dress (to blend with the gray and yellow tones in the sky) over black leggings and metallic-silver ballet flats. Nature was her only style guide that morning, because she had zero clue where she was being taken—or why.

Would Skye really be there in eight seconds, or was the pizza message another one of the DSL Daters' jokes?

But at exactly 1 p.m., the familiar sounds of tires crunched over the Blocks' circular gravel driveway.

Massie released the curtains and ducked.

Now what? Race outside to show Skye she, too, was punctual? Or hang back and wait for the doorbell to ring? Luckily, two short blasts of a car horn made the decision for her.

"'Bye, Mom," Massie called as she hurried to the tall double doors.

"When will you be back?" Kendra Block's smooth, post-yoga voice oozed from the tiny white intercom in the corner of the ceiling.

"Before dark," Massie guessed, hoping she was right.

"Who are you going out with?"

"Skye Hamilton." Massie checked her reflection in the brass door handle. Thankfully, her new Bumble and Bumble hairspray was hard at work, holding her long, side-swept bangs in place over her left eye. "You don't know her—she's in the eighth grade."

"Daisy Hamilton's daughter?"

"Um, yeah?" Massie turned the knob and stepped outside before her mother could ask any more questions she didn't know the answers to. "I'm on my cell if you need me. 'Byeeeeee."

"Are you wearing a coat?"

Massie quickly slammed the door behind her.

A pine-green Toyota Prius was waiting with the engine running and the stereo blasting Jack Johnson's "Upside Down." Skye waved from the passenger seat, flashing a wide, toothy BFF smile, even though this was the first time they'd ever hung out on a weekend.

Massie opened the door and slid in beside a pink child's seat littered with graham cracker crumbs. A nauseating tangy citrus smell wafted off the orange cardboard happy face dangling from the rearview mirror. Was it too late to suggest they take the Range Rover?

"Welcome," cooed the laid-back high school guy behind the wheel. "My Christian name is Jarrett, but my friends call me Leaf." He swiped his shoulder-length butterscotch-colored hair to the left side of his neck. His round, yellow-lensed sunglasses and tweed blazer were a little too wannabe-sensitive-poet for Massie's taste, and she couldn't help thinking how cute he would look after a Josh Hartnett cut and a trip to Hollister.

"Leaf and I met at a dance-a-thon last Christmas," Skye offered. "He was dancing to raise money for poor parents who couldn't afford to buy Christmas presents, and I was dancing to burn calories before a big jazz showcase I had the next morning. We bonded over Ciara."

Leaf chuckled at the memory.

"Nice to meet you," Massie responded, feeling a little jumpy, like one of those characters in mob movies who are ordered into the back of a Lincoln Town Car and forced to make small talk while being driven to the waterfront, where they inevitably get shot.

"So." Her voice quaked. "What's the plan?"

Skye nodded at Leaf, who then screeched out of the driveway. "You'lllll seeeee," she cooed in a playful singsong voice.

Massie leaned forward, hoping a glimpse at Skye's outfit might tip her off as to their destination. As usual, Skye was dressed in something from her parents' upscale dancewear boutique. This time it was a tight light pink three-quarter-sleeve ballet crop top. Khaki jodhpurs and black riding boots put an unexpected jockey-chic spin on the outfit, heightening Massie's curiosity about their afternoon plans even more.

"Can you believe we only have, like, three weeks left of school?" Skye asked her reflection in the side mirror as she straightened her double-wire headband and tightened her butter-blond chignon.

"You private school girls have it made." Leaf slapped the steering wheel like it wasn't fair. "You get, like, four months off. I swear, the more money you pay for school, the less you have to go."

"We're supposed to use that time to educate ourselves in the real world," Skye said with a smile, like she knew what a joke that was.

"And how are you educating yourself?" Leaf took off his glasses and glared at her, full of mock doubt.

"I'm taking extra ballet classes in May and then going to South Beach with Isabella's family for a month. Then when I get back it's straight to NYC to register for dance school."

"Very educational." Leaf slid his round glasses back on. "And you, Massie?" he asked her reflection in the rearview mirror.

"Hanging by my pool with the Pretty Committee. Then in June I go to riding camp at Galwaugh Farms." Massie purposely sounded blasé to let Skye know that her long-standing membership at the exclusive stables was no big deal, even though it so was.

She waited for a reaction. Something like, "Ehmagawd, you have to be such a good rider to get into that camp." Or "I heard they only let billionaires join." But unfortunately, Skye didn't have a single envious word to say, which made Massie love/hate her even more.

"What about you?" Massie politely asked Leaf, as they turned down Shadow Lane, the winding tree-lined road that led to Galwaugh Farms. She really didn't care what Leaf was doing this summer. It was more about showing Skye she wasn't afraid to talk to older guys.

"I'm going to Peru to build a health clinic out of mud, straw, and pebbles."

Massie burst out laughing, grateful for Leaf's dark sense of humor. His joke eased her rattled nerves.

"What's so funny?" He turned toward the backseat.

Massie's cheeks burned. Before she could come up with a decent reason for laughing at his earnest charity work, Skye interjected.

"See?" She mussed his long, butterscotch-colored hair. "I'm not the only one who thinks building a health clinic will take more than *one* summer."

Massie leaned her forehead against the window, using the chilly glass to cool her flaming cheeks. Was there something wrong with her for thinking Leaf's summer plan—building clinics out of mud, straw, and pebbles—was a *joke*? Skye ah-bviously though it was cool. Why didn't *she*? Massie was overcome with a sudden longing for the Pretty Committee, because they would have found it hard to believe too. She shut her eyes and waited for the loneliness to pass.

When she opened them, they were rolling under the log archway to Galwaugh Farms. The Prius stopped at the log security hut.

"Member number." The guard leaned inside the driver's-side window.

Leaf and Skye turned to face Massie. She blushed again.

"Member number?" Skye insisted.

Massie scooted forward and waved. "Hi, Pat."

"Oh, hi, Miss Block." His wrinkled face wrinkled more when he smiled. "Didn't see you back there. Go 'head." He waved them through.

Massie breathed in the familiar smell of horse poo and hay. Was Skye using her to get into the exclusive riding club? It was hard to know for sure, because Massie had never been *used* before. What were the signs? And if this whole "U-thing"really was happening, maybe it would be possible to use Skye back. She ah-bviously wanted something Massie had. And Skye had plenty of things Massie wanted. The situation had definite potential.

"So, what are we doing here?"

"You'llll seeeee," Skye singsonged again.

Leaf parked in the dusty lot and turned off the engine.

"Thanks." Skye handed him a Hershey's Kiss, her signature way of thanking high school boys for rides. "We should be done here in an hour."

"Take your time." Leaf pulled out a black sketchbook and a stick of charcoal from his wheat-colored hemp messenger bag.

"So where's your horse?" Skye asked, once the two of them were away from the car.

"Stable B. Why?"

Skye consulted her pink pigskin Coach watch. "Can we be there in three minutes?"

Massie nodded, suddenly overwhelmed by guilt. It was the first time she had ever set foot on the farm without bringing star-shaped carrots for Brownie.

"Why are we here?" she tried again.

"You'lllll seeeee."

Something inside Massie suddenly snapped. If she didn't muster up some self-respect soon, it would be all over school Monday that she'd let Skye drag her around like a cheap Samsonite.

"Tell me or we're not going." She dug her metallic ballet flats into the dirt. So what if Skye was the eighth-grade alpha at OCD? They weren't at OCD; they were at Galwaugh. And here, *she* was the alpha.

Skye checked her watch again. "Fine, but let's walk."

"Fine." Massie smoothed her silver-and-gold dress, then led the way down the stone walkway toward the stables. "Now *tell* me."

Skye pulled a gold heart-shaped locket out from her modest cleavage. "I got this from Chris Abeley almost a week ago." She paused, obviously waiting for a reaction. "And I haven't heard from him since."

But Massie gave her nothing. Her mouth was too dry to speak. If Skye found out the necklace had not been a love gift from Chris Abeley but, instead a cheap trinket that had once belonged to his LBR sister, Layne, she'd kick Massie back to the first grade.

Skye tugged the chain. "It came with a note."

"Really? A note?" Massie did her best to sound surprised, even though she knew exactly what it said. After all, she'd written it herself as part of her desperate scheme to win Skye's key competition.

"Yeah." She pulled a worn piece of paper out of the thin back pocket of her khaki jodhpurs and unfolded it. She looked over her shoulder, then leaned in toward Massie and read it aloud.

SKYE,
  HERE is the pony you asked for. ONE
day I hope I can get you the REAL thing.
                 HAPPY graduation,
                 xo Chris Abeley
  PS-PLEASE don't thank me. EVER! I REAlly
mean it! PLEASE don't! I'm VERy, VERy shy.

"Pony?" Massie asked, purposely sounding dumb to keep her cover. "I thought he got you a necklace."

Skye grabbed her wrist and pulled Massie behind a thick oak tree, as if they were being watched. She cupped a hand around her mouth and whispered, "Remember when you came to my house during the key competition?"

Massie bit her tongue, afraid that even the slightest sound might give her away.

"And remember how I thought you were there to find out where I'd hidden the key, but you said you were there because Chris sent you over to find out what I wanted for graduation?"

Massie nodded. Her armpits flooded with sweat as she remembered using that pathetic excuse. It was still hard to believe Skye bought it. Or had she?

"I said I wanted a pony, remember?"

Massie nodded again. The faint smell of her baby-powder-scented Secret deodorant quickly came and went.

"And you must have told him that, right?" Skye asked, her blue eyes wide.

"Um, yup," Massie answered.

"Well, you know how shy he is, right?"

Massie nodded in agreement.

"So there I was at a soccer game, when some fifth-grader taps me on the shoulder and gives me *this*—"

While Skye struggled to open the clasp on the locket, Massie smiled at the memory of asking Todd Lyons, Claire's little brother, to deliver the necklace and making him promise to say it was from Chris. Her plan had been so elaborate it was hard to believe it had actually worked. Unless, of course, Skye knew she had been tricked and had brought her to the woods to—

The locket popped open.

"How cute!" The eighth-grade alpha flashed it in front of Massie's face. "Look inside. There's a picture of Tricky, Chris's horse. That's the *pony* he gave me for graduation. Is that clever or is that clever?"

"Cle-ver," Massie managed as she fake-studied the photo of the all-black horse she had carefully snipped from the *Galwaugh Farms Register.*

"Sooo *totally* clever, right?"

"So totally clever."

"And cute."

"Totally cute."

"Then why hasn't he texted me?" Skye whined. "He signed his name with an 'xo.' Doesn't that mean he likes me?"

Massie shrug-nodded, her tongue temporarily swollen with fear. Was Skye testing her? Giving her the chance to come clean on the fake gift? Were the DSL Daters hiding behind the bushes waiting for an attack signal?

"So what's the problem?" Massie tried to steady her voice.

"I want him to be my date for the costume party," Skye continued. "But he hasn't called me and I *can't* call him. That's way too desperate."

Massie nodded impatiently. "So why are we *here*?"

All of a sudden, Skye gripped her arm, silently urging Massie to stop. "Look." She pointed at Stable B.

Chris Abeley was leading Tricky onto the trail. He was wearing a dark gray bomber jacket and a navy knit snowboarding cap. Wisps of scruffy brown hair poked out the sides and blew in the light breeze. There was no need to question the reason for Skye's crush—he was a walking Abercrombie bag.

"How did you know he'd be—"

"Say hi," Skye whisper-begged. "Act like it's a coincidence."

"But—"

"Hurry, before he gets too far."

"Um, hey, Chris!" Massie squeaked, and then waved awkwardly, a second later than she should have.

He turned, lifted his palm, and flashed his Crest Whitestrip smile—the same one that had made Massie obsess over him eight months earlier when they'd met riding on this very trail. If it hadn't been for Fawn, his tall, honey-blond, genetically perfect high school ex-girlfriend—*current* girlfriend at the time—Chris would have been Massie's HART, and Derrington would have been just another seventh-grade boy who admired her from afar.

"Let's go." Skye hurried toward him.

Massie had no choice but to follow.

"Awwww, look at that cute horsey." Skye hugged Tricky's long black neck. "I just love animals. Love love love love love!"

Chris smiled politely, then turned to Massie. His use of DEC (direct eye contact) filled her with such intense tingles she wanted to sprint. Her crush was making a bigger come-back than Cadillac.

"Didn't we first meet here?" he asked, his dark blue eyes crinkling fondly at the memory.

"Yup." Massie nodded to her metallic flats in a desperate attempt to escape his knee-weakening gaze. "You tried to run me off the trail."

"Yeah, but you showed me, didn't you?"

She found the courage to meet his eyes again. "No one beats me to Hunter Lake."

"How 'bout we try again in a few months? I signed up for camp this summer just so I could kick your—"

"No way!" Massie interrupted. "I'm going to camp here too."

Chris bit his lower lip, cocked his head, and half-smiled. His hawtness was like an invisible force field that drew her in and held her. And to think he'd come from the same womb as LBR Layne.

"Ech-hem." Skye pinched the back of Massie's arm.

"Oh." Massie stiffened. "And, um, Skye is taking dance and then going to South Beach."

"And then New York City," she bragged. "I got into a performing arts high school."

He smile-nodded like someone trying hard to care. Not like someone who supposedly had a crush on Skye but was too shy to tell her. Massie speed-searched her brain for a way to keep her elaborate scheme from unraveling but found it hard to focus on anything other than the navy-blueness of Chris Abeley's eyes.

Skye rocked on the heels of her riding boots and slid the gold locket across its chain.

"My sister has the same necklace," he offered.

"Rea-lly?" Skye winked, as if that were code for *"Thank you, I love my gift."*

Massie's stomach felt like it did when she jumped hurdles with Brownie. Was Skye about to openly acknowledge the locket to Chris?

Chris's eyebrows crinkled in confusion, obviously questioning what Skye was talking about.

A crisp pre-spring breeze rustled the leaves on the massive tree above their heads, and Massie looked up with feigned interest—anything to avoid his suspicious gaze.

"So, what brings you guys here?" he asked.

Massie lowered her head and side-glanced at Skye, silent-begging her to interject, which, of course, she did.

"*J'adore* horses." She lifted the locket to her lips and kissed it. "Simple as that."

Massie admired her confidence, which made her want access to the secret room and ESP even more. She imagined herself a year from now, standing with Chris and making *him* sweat and stammer. Not the other way around. Like a super-hero with special powers, Massie Block would become . . . the Heartless HART-breaker.

"I know what you mean." Chris kicked the dirt with his black Timberland hiking boots. "I don't know what I would do without my girl." He affectionately smacked his horse's rump. "She's my one and only."

"That can't be true." Skye smiled, a combination of hope and disappointment clouding her eyes. "Can it?"

"These days it is." Chris finger-combed Tricky's mane. "Ever since Fawn and I broke . . ." His voice trailed off. He shook a memory from his head and then found his way back to a lighthearted smile. "Point is, I'm never gonna let myself get hurt again. I'm over girls." He slipped his foot into a stirrup and hopped on his horse. "Except for one." He looked at Massie, but love-tapped Tricky. "I better go." And with a snap of the reins, they were off. "See ya!" he shouted without looking back.

The girls watched in silence as he disappeared down the trail, leaving them in a cloud of dust and desire.

Skye clutched the locket and shook her head in confusion. "Let's get out of here."

"Don't you want to meet Brownie? She's white and—"

"Nah." Skye angled her feet in third position and sulked up the stone path. "If he's so over girls, why did he give me this locket?"

Massie, having no idea how to answer that question without getting into trouble, placed a reassuring hand on Skye's sharp shoulder blade and sighed. "Maybe you don't understand boys as well as you thought you did."

Skye stopped to consider this. "Impossible." She lifted her chin. "I bet he was acting that way because *you* were there. And he didn't want you to feel left out."

"Probably," Massie managed. But she would have said anything, no matter how false, to keep Skye from discovering the truth.

"Well, you seem to know him pretty well," Skye snipped.

"Not really, I just—"

"Will you make him call me so I can invite him to my party?"

"How am I supposed to do *that*?" Massie asked as they approached the parking lot. "He's sworn off girls, remember?"

"Well, get him to swear back on them."

The level of desperation in Skye's watery turquoise eyes shocked Massie. She had never seen an alpha act like such a beta before.

And then Massie grinned.

"You'll do it?" Skye beamed.

"Of course." She shrugged, like it was no big deal.

Skye threw her arms around her, flooding the air with the heady floral smell of Aveda's Shampure. It was weird seeing an alpha express her need for help so openly. It was something Massie had never realized alphas were allowed to do.

Skye pulled away but kept a firm grip on Massie's shoulders.

"You're the best. I'm so—"

"On one condition."

Skye's smile faded, just as a cloud covered the sun. A chill stung the air, and Massie suddenly wished she'd brought her Marc Jacobs cropped denim jacket.

"What's your condition?" Skye asked suspiciously.

"Give me access to the room *this* year." Massie fought to keep her voice measured and calm. "I want ESP ASAP."

"Impressive." Skye sized Massie up as if seeing her for the first time. "Nice negotiating skills. You *are* an alpha."

Massie couldn't help herself and grinned with pride.

"Will you make Chris contact me?"

"Will you give me the room?"

"Contact?"

"Room?"

"Contact?"

"Room?"

They stood, inches away from the pine-green Prius, locked in a stare-down.

Skye's eyes scanned Massie's Ella Moss dress, landed on her metallic shoes, and then floated back up to her glossy side-part. More than anything, Massie wanted to hand-check her bangs, but she knew the gesture would make her look insecure, so she left them to fate.

Finally, Skye raised her pinky. "Deal."

Massie's heart leapt.

"You can have it for forty-five minutes twice a week, when the seventh-graders have their class."

"Deal!" Massie couldn't *wait* to tell the Pretty Committee how she'd manipulated Skye and gotten them access to the room *months* ahead of schedule. She reached for Skye's baby finger.

"Not so fast."

"Why?" Massie's pinky hung in the air.

"If Chris isn't my date for the party—"

"Wait, you said contact, nawt *date*."

But Skye didn't seem too concerned with semantics. "If Chris isn't my actual d-a-t-e for the party, I'm taking the room back. Deal?"

She wiggled her pinky.

Massie stared at it.

Slipping Skye a necklace "from Chris" was one thing, but actually making him go to Skye's own costume party as her *date* was quite another. Could she make him forget his ex and like a new girl in less than two weeks? And was she willing to lose the room if she couldn't?

Skye wiggled her pinky again. Massie continued to stare at it, as she silently asked herself a series of hard-hitting and very important questions.

Q: Could she pull this off?

She thought back to the time she'd stopped Claire's dad from moving the family to Chicago. And when she'd persuaded *Teen Vogue* to do a holiday photo shoot with the Pretty Committee. And when she'd opened a kissing clinic, even though she was a total lip-virgin.

A: Massie Block always found a way to get her way. *Always*.

Q: And if she didn't?

A: Skye would lock them out of the room and the girls would have to find dates the old-fashioned way.

Q: Then what?

A: They'd be in eighth grade and the room would be theirs anyway.

Q: And that was all that really mattered, right?

A: Right. A private meeting spot, 24/7 ESP access, and membership into the secret alpha club would make the eighth grade the best year ever.

Q: So what was she waiting for?

A: Nuh-*thing*!

Massie thrust her finger toward Skye's and shook.

Skye reached into her ballerina-pink training bra and pulled out a single gold key. She slapped it in Massie's palm, then insisted, "Repeat the deal back to me."

Massie rolled her eyes, letting Skye know she didn't appreciate being treated like a fifth-grader.

"If Chris is not your date, you're taking the room back until next year."

"WRONG!"

"What?"

"For *good*." Skye tightened her grip. "I'm taking the room back for *good*."

"Forget it." Massie yanked her finger away. "No deal."

"Too late. You shook."

Massie was tempted to argue but knew Skye was right. A pinky swear was binding. Every alpha knew *that*.

Leaf backed the Prius out of its parking spot and pulled up beside the girls. With a single click, the doors unlocked, and Skye lowered herself onto the front bucket seat. She smiled brightly and Massie tried to do the same. But it was impossible. Even though there hadn't been any mobsters, and no one had gotten shot, she couldn't help feeling that life, as she knew it, was over.

The Pretty Committee giggle-panted as they scurried bare-foot down the cold, dimly lit flight of stairs that led to OCD's boiler room. Clutching their flats so they wouldn't make too much noise, their bare feet slapping against the floor, they ran past the huge clanging cylinders that pumped steam or air or water or something into the school, and yanked open the door marked CAUTION: DO NOT ENTER.

"More? Gawd, where *are* we?" Alicia huffed when she saw the narrow gray steps with the wobbly thin black railing. "Are we below sea level yet?"

"Shhhhh!" everyone giggle-hissed.

Massie pointed to the moist dark ceiling, reminding them that Principal Burns's office was only two floors above. Silently, they followed her down to the basement below the basement, toward the bomb shelter.

Claire scanned the dank halls for faculty, while Massie fumbled with the key. It was nothing short of a miracle that Mr. Myner, their tree-hugging geography teacher, had given his class twenty minutes of unsupervised time to collect mud samples from the garden. To him, the assignment was a clever way of demonstrating to his class how varying degrees of sun exposure can affect the quality of soil, but for the Pretty

Committee it was the perfect opportunity to sneak into The Room.

"Got it!" Massie finally announced, her ivory-yarn-covered hoop earrings swinging as she turned the silver handle. "Let's move!"

The girls slid their flats back on, hurried inside, and then quickly but quietly shut the black door behind them.

The bitter-rich aroma of fresh coffee mixed with a trace amount of floral perfume welcomed them when they entered.

"Eh," gushed Alicia.

"Ma," followed Dylan.

"Gawd!" finished Kristen.

"Now *this* is my idea of a secret room!" Massie's arched eyebrows were raised, her amber eyes wide.

The girls split up instantly to explore.

"Is this a *real* Starbucks machine?" Claire stroked the shiny brass body of the massive espresso maker that was on the top tier of an elegant rolling tea service, to the right of the entrance. The glass shelf below was piled high with the company's signature green-and-white cardboard to-go cups; pink, yellow, and blue packets of sweeteners; sugar cubes; and powdered milk for the steamer. She pushed the cart like a baby in a stroller, while following Massie to the monitor.

"I'm all over *this*." Alicia was still by the entrance, standing in front of a chrome-and-mirrored vanity. The white marble counter space was covered in what had to be every color of nail polish, eyeliner (glitter and plain), gloss, and shadow ever made by Hard Candy. The rubber rings that came on the bottles of polish had been strung like popcorn and draped over the top of the mirror.

"Iss op-orn is ate," Dylan said, chewing a mouthful of popcorn she had taken from the movie-theater-size dispenser. "Ust the right amount of utter."

"ESP, anyone?" Massie sat, kicked off her Tory Burch leopard-print flats, and then dipped her stairwell-dirty feet in a swirling-soapy-bubble-filled foot massager.

"You *have* to see these racks," Kristen gasped, obviously shocked that such an incredible collection of designer clothes and shoes had been entrusted to them. "They have more than fifteen different Puma track jackets." She slid the wood hangers across the shiny silver garment pole. "I've never seen this green limited-edition one with the peacock feathers, have you?"

"No," they all gasped with a mix of shock and delight.

Claire bit her pinky nail.

Technically, she was just as excited as the others. But they had been gone for six minutes, and Mr. Myner was probably starting to wonder where they were. She bit down on her nail again. "Maybe we should come back tomorrow. The period is almost over, and none of us have any soil samples."

Dylan lifted her head out of a picnic basket by the popcorn maker. "There'll be one in your Jockeys any minute now if you don't relax."

Claire ignored the jab while the others cracked up. She put the Starbucks cart aside and began pacing.

"Kuh-laire, what would you rather?" Massie lifted a dripping foot out of the massager and crossed her legs. Bubbles slid off her YSL brick-red polish and landed on the floor with a splat. "A lecture from Mr. Myner about wandering off without permission, or to be renamed the Cheetah Girls because we'll be the only ones at Skye's eighth-grade party without HARTs?"

"But I already have a boy—"

"Um, last time I checked we were the Pretty Committee, nawt the Pretty *Claire*."

"Sorry." Claire apologized and meant it. "You're right."

"As usual." Massie dipped her toes back in the swirling foot spa.

"Ehmagawd, you guys?" Dylan called, her head back in the basket. "I bet there's more than fifty different types of seasoning in here. And they're all for the popcorn." She snapped off a stiff corner of one of the edible candy snack bags and popped it in her mouth. "And these are de-*lish*." She lifted her emerald-green eyes to the ceiling and licked her lips while contemplating the bag's flavor. "Butterscotch?"

"Massie, check out these iridescent eye shadows," Alicia squealed in delight. "I heard Paris Hilton bought the entire collection."

"We have all of next year for that." Massie nodded toward the blank monitor. "Right now we're on a HART hunt."

"Point." Alicia tore herself away from the vanity and made her way, along with Kristen and Dylan, toward the pink faux-fur seats. "Ew!" she mused, stepping over a slew of empty lip-gloss-stained Starbucks venti cups. *Teen Vogue* magazine subscription cards, balled silver gum wrappers, and half-popped popcorn kernels were scattered across the pink shag area rug. "The DSL Daters are even messier than Dylan!"

A kernel smacked against Alicia's zit-free forehead and Dylan burst out laughing. "Ooops, sorry."

Alicia picked up a wood coffee stirrer off the floor and poked Dylan's yellow-and-brown-plaid Western shirt, straight through to her fleshy bicep. "Ouch!"

Dylan tugged Alicia's low black side-pony and let out a *"toot, toooooot!"* Her impersonation of a ship's horn was an obvious a reference to Alicia's navy-and-white-striped boat-neck sailor dress.

"Let's hope we got us the right class schedule." Massie aimed the pink-Swarovski-crystal-covered remote at the flat-screen TV and pressed POWER. "Here we go."

Claire forced her jittery legs into the chair. Technically, this was worse than journal reading, and she couldn't help feeling that somehow Cam would sense that she was spying.

The others took their seats just as a black-and-white image appeared on the screen.

"Eh," said Alicia.

"Ma," said Dylan.

"Gawd!" said Kristen.

"It works," whisper-gasped Massie in awe. She shut off the noisy foot massager, letting her feet wade in the sudsy still water.

A semicircle of fifteen desks, each one occupied by a different Briarwood boy, flickered back at them.

Immediately, Claire scanned the room for Cam. He was sitting a few seats away from the window, next to Derrington, listening to some boy with a buzz cut who was in the middle of a rant. She shielded her eyes in case there was any possible way he could see her.

". . . It's like she swears I'm thinking certain things when I'm not thinking anything at all," said Buzz Cut Boy.

"No way!" Alicia gasped. "That's Miles Burke, Bella's crush. She was crying about him today in the bathroom because she said he's been ignoring her!"

"Shhhhh!" the girls snapped in unison, not taking their eyes off the screen.

"What kinds of things does she think you're thinking?" boomed a deep, older male voice with a faint Southern accent.

"Ehmagawd, it's Dr. Loni," squealed Dylan. "He sounds just like he does on the radio."

"Shhhhhhhh!" the girls snapped again.

"I dunno." Miles bit the side of his pencil. "Like, last night I was supposed to call her and I didn't, so today I get this text that says she thinks I have intimacy issues because my parents just got divorced."

"Well?" Dr. Loni asked, expectantly.

"Well, *what?*" huffed Miles. "I didn't call her back because her number was written on the side of my Nikes and my Nikes were in my room."

"And?" asked the radio host, not quite getting the connection.

"*And* I was in the attic playing Formula One with my brother and our cousin."

The boys snickered, like they totally understood his position.

"Why didn't you call her *after* the game?"

"I figured we'd talk today or something. And now she's mad at me." Miles shrugged.

"Would you call that a lack of communication?" the man-voice prompted him.

"No, I'd call it psycho."

Cam laughed with the rest of the boys, giving Claire an instant ache in her stomach, her legs, her temples, and her heart. She would have expected Cam to understand Bella's point of view, not mock it. Had her seemingly sensitive crush always been such a guy's guy?

The laughter died and Cam tapped a Bic pen against his Nikki notebook. It was then Claire realized that maybe she'd never really known him at all.

"Let's move to today's topic," boomed Dr. Loni, from somewhere beyond the camera's reach. "It's called, 'You're Only as Sick as Your Secrets.'"

For the next few seconds, all the girls heard was chalk tapping against the blackboard.

Cam's eyes were fixed on what must have been the Share Bear, because it looked like he was staring straight at Claire.

"Am I the only one who thinks this is kinda creepy?" she asked.

The Pretty Committee was too mesmerized to respond.

"Why don't we start with Josh," suggested Dr. Loni. "Josh, what emotions have been holding you hostage this week?"

Suddenly the camera shook and swayed. Bumpy shots of the cookies-'n'-cream-colored linoleum floor and the white tips of a man's Reeboks filled the frame. The camera steadied on one of Josh's wide brown eyes, which, as usual, was shaded by the brim of his New York Yankees hat.

Claire's heart thumped again, like it was trying to warn her. "Maybe we should rethink this."

"Easy for you to say," Massie snapped. "You already have a date for Skye's party."

"So do you!"

"Yeah, but *they* don't." Massie gestured to Alicia, Dylan, and Kristen, who nodded in agreement. "And Skye said we all have to have dates or we'll be paci-fired."

"Paci Block," Dylan burped.

Everyone burst out laughing except Claire.

"You don't get it." She ripped open the Velcro side pocket on her cocoa-colored cargos. "I just think this whole spying thing is wrong. It's like reading someone's journal or wiretapping their phone."

"What's wrong with *that*?" Dylan asked with sincerity.

"Claire has a point." Kristen twirled the laces of her green-and-khaki Burton camo sneakers around her finger. "It's an invasion of privacy."

Claire smile-thanked her and continued with newfound courage. "How would you like it if someone read your e-mail?"

"Impossible, it's password-protected," Dylan replied, oozing "duh."

"Hey, are you guys super-tall jockeys?" Massie asked.

Claire and Kristen shook their heads no.

"Then get off your high horses."

Dylan and Alicia jumped down from their chairs to high-five Massie.

The Share Bear shifted in Josh's grip, revealing a quick shot of Griffin Hastings. Black choppy hair flopped over his eyes as he secretly read a mysterious paperback under his desk.

"Ehmagawd." Kristen rushed to the monitor and practically flattened her nose against the screen. "Was that my busboy?"

"Yup," Massie, Dylan, and Alicia confirmed.

"Was he *reading* in class?"

"Yup," they answered.

Claire's mouth dried up. She was about to lose her only ally.

"I'm so calling dibs on him." Kristen opened her arms, hugged the sides of the TV, and kissed it, leaving behind a glossy lip-print. "Invasion-of-privacy issues are *so* three minutes ago."

"Great. Kristen is done." Massie tapped a note into her PalmPilot. "Alicia and Dylan, I need you to focus. Think 'alpha male.'"

Alicia pulled out her hair elastic and shot it at Kristen's back. "Move! Josh is about to share."

Claire lowered her head into her hands, vowing to keep herself shrouded in darkness until this crime against morality was over. She caught a glimpse of her pink Baby G-Shock watch. The bell was about to ring. Mr. Myner *had* to be wondering where they were by now.

"Since when do you care about *Josh*?" Dylan ran a hand along one of her thick red braids. "Back when we were searching under boys' mattresses for the key to this bomb shelter, you said his bedroom was freaky clean in a turnoff sort of way."

"It is," Alicia agreed. "But a secret's a secret. I don't care *who* it belongs to, my ears wanna hear it. Besides, I've been low on gossip points this month."

"Go ahead," urged Dr. Loni's voice from the flat-screen's surround sound. "It's safe."

The sudden, high-pitched screech of metal probably meant the boys were shifting uncomfortably in their seats.

Claire spread her fingers, just enough to get a narrow peek at the TV screen.

"Well . . ." Josh paused, his finger circling the eye of the Share Bear and blocking their view. "Sometimes I boss my sister around when my parents aren't home."

Dr. Loni cleared his throat. "And by this you mean . . ."

"I mean I kidnap her Bratz dolls and dangle them over the disposal until she does my chores." He stopped circling the eye and lowered his head in shame. "Stuff like that."

"Geeeenius!" Derrington leaned across Cam to high-five Josh.

"Nice shorts." Massie rolled her eyes when she saw his tiger-striped surf trunks. "Gawd, why can't he ever be serious?"

"Derek!" snapped Dr. Loni, who finally appeared in the shot. A rectangle of sunlight cut across his bald head like a giant Band-Aid. He had skinny legs and a thick midsection, which he tried to cover with a loose velour tracksuit. "You're eroding our fortress of trust." He stroked his close-cut goatee, stomped out of the frame, and disappeared.

"Sorry." Derrington made a show of lifting his butt and sitting on his naughty hand. He knocked his bare knees together like a hyperactive child.

"Josh," continued Dr. Loni, "how does it make you feel when your sister does your chores?"

Josh's head stayed down. "Good at first, 'cause, you know, my chores are done and I didn't have to do them."

"Good, good. And then?"

"And then kinda bad, 'cause while I'm playing Xbox, she's upstairs cleaning my room."

"Do you think next time you could resist the urge to kidnap, and do the chores yourself?" asked Dr. Loni.

Josh shrugged, like he was seriously contemplating this.

"Ehmagawd, *she* cleans his room!" Alicia bobbed in her seat. "He's nawt freakishly clean—*she* is. My crush is back."

Massie stamped her fist on the arm of her pink chair. "Ah-pproved."

"Wait," Claire couldn't help interjecting. "Doesn't it bother you that he's so mean to his sister? Do you think Skye would find that *suitable*?"

"Point," Alicia sighed.

Massie highlighted something on her PalmPilot and hit DELETE. "Thanks a lot," she mouthed to Claire.

"Would anyone else like to share?" asked Dr. Loni.

"I have a question." Kemp Hurley raised his hand. "If girls don't want to hook up, why do they dress like they do?"

The boys whooped and hollered.

Claire checked her pink Baby G-Shock watch again. "I'm gonna get some soil."

She knew this sudden show of morality would land her on Massie's "out" list for at least a week—not that she cared. If Massie hadn't encouraged her to flirt, she never would have read Cam's journal. And if she hadn't read the journal, she never would have skipped class to try and get the Nikki scoop. Not that she'd gotten any. The only thing she *had* gotten was more confusion and guilt.

Claire turned the door handle.

"Maybe Cam should *share* what happened at Slice of Heaven last week," said one of the boys. It sounded like Derrington.

She whipped her head around. Close-up black-and-white shots of hands passing the Share Bear down the row of seats filled the screen.

"What?" Cam's voice cracked, in the same desperate way it had when he was begging Claire to turn over the notebook at Slice of Heaven. "Nothing happened."

Staring at the side of his square jaw and the collar of his worn leather jacket, Claire wondered how someone she knew so well could suddenly feel like such a stranger.

"Looks like someone fell off her high horse." Dylan snickered when she saw Claire return to her seat.

Claire was too riveted to respond.

All she could do was watch the screen and try to steady her breath while Cam worked up the courage to share his big secret: his love affair with Nikki.

"Would it be easier if you read from your journal?" asked Dr. Loni in his sensitive Southern accent.

"No." Cam shifted nervously. He lifted his knees to his chest, hugged them, and then lowered his legs in an obvious attempt to find comfort in an uncomfortable situation.

The class waited in silence.

Claire's palms started to sweat. *What was he so anxious about?*

"Just tell him about the cinnamon hearts," Derrington insisted.

"Dude!" Cam snapped.

Claire grabbed the crystal-covered remote from Massie's warm grip and turned up the volume.

"Looks like someone is getting *trampled* by her high horse." Massie smirked.

"Point." Alicia lifted her finger.

"This doesn't count." Claire heard her voice shake. "He's talking about *my* present. It's personal."

"Was there another gift, Cam?" Dr. Loni asked, obviously trying to move the discussion forward.

"Yeah," he answered, his voice dripping with shame.

"What's wrong with the gifts?" Claire pleaded with the screen, like her mother did when she watched *The Young and the Restless*. "What's wrong with the *gifts*?"

"I think you mean *re*-gifts," Derrington joked.

The boys snickered.

The girls gasped.

"Re-gifts?" Claire screeched. "What's *that* supposed to mean?"

"Why don't you mind your own business?" Cam shook his fist at Derrington.

It was the first time Claire had ever seen Cam lose his temper.

"Relax," Derrington urged. "I'm just trying to help you *share*." He made air quotes when he said "share."

Massie giggled, obviously taking pleasure in Derrington's ability to provoke Cam.

"Why don't you help *yourself* share." Cam suddenly whipped the bear at him. A dizzying blur dominated the screen. The girls looked away with a collective moan.

"Why don't you tell Dr. Loni about your big *issue* with Massie?" they heard Cam say as someone lifted the bear off the floor. The camera settled on a close-up of pale skin and light blond hair.

"Look, it's Derrington's thigh." Dylan giggled.

"Ew!" Alicia covered her brown eyes.

"Quiet!" Massie jumped to her feet, splashing soapy foot-spa water all over the black rubber floor. "He has an *issue* with me?"

"Wait!" Claire shouted. "Go back to the re-gifting thing."

"What's the *issue*?" Massie wailed at Derrington's thigh.

"It's your turn to share, not mine," his voice insisted.

"Then why do *you* have the bear?" Cam jeered.

"I don't!" A speedy pan of blurry faces flashed across the monitor as Derrington chucked the bear across the room. It landed on the floor beside someone's navy Timbuk2 messenger bag.

"That's enough!" Dr. Loni clapped twice from somewhere in the room. With a light grunt, he bent down and retrieved the bear. "Would anyone else like to talk about Slice of Heaven before we move on?"

"Move *on*?" Massie and Claire shouted at the same time.

As if hearing their cries, Dr. Loni explained, "We'll get back to Cam and Derek once they find the courage to face their emotions. Does *anyone* feel brave enough to share?"

"I do." Chris Plovert slowly lifted his hand.

The girls shut their eyes as the Share Bear made another nauseating journey across the row of seats.

"Thanks." Plovert smiled shyly as he clutched the bear. Its eyes pointed straight at the slight bump on the bridge of his nose, where his round glasses clamped on like a koala. "Um, I just wanted to say something about Dylan Marvil."

"Ha!" Alicia smacked Dylan's faded ultra-vintage Levi's. "I told you not to eat!"

Dylan lips parted in horror but no sound emerged.

"It's safe," assured Dr. Loni. "Go on."

The girls slid out of their chairs and inched closer to the monitor.

"I kinda think she's cool." Plovert pushed up his glasses, even though they weren't slipping.

"Awwww, yeah!" Dylan punched the sky. She looked at Massie, then Alicia, then Kristen. But each girl acted as though they hadn't heard his endearing confession. Claire was the only one who returned her enthusiasm with a halfhearted air-clap.

"I think she's cool too," Kemp Hurley chimed in. "She's like the only chick I've ever seen eat. It's hot."

"Exactly," Plovert exclaimed. "She's fun."

"Exactly," agreed Kemp. "Like a guy, but hot."

"Really hot."

"Awwww, yeah!" Dylan kicked up her legs.

Alicia and Massie curled their upper lips in disgust and rolled their eyes.

"Mr. Plovert has the bear, not you," Dr. Loni reminded Kemp.

"Sorry."

"Ha!" Dylan leaned over and playfully tugged Alicia's side-pony. "So much for not eating till I'm married."

"Are you sure they meant you and not me?" Alicia whimpered.

Dylan widened her green eyes in disbelief.

"No offense." Alicia placed a kind hand on her friend's shoulder. "It's just that these guys are usually crushing on me and—"

"And today they're nawt." Dylan turned away. "Chew on that! Oops, sorry, I forgot. You don't *eat*!"

"When I write about her in my journal"—Plovert pushed up his glasses again—"I call her Marvil-ous, you know, 'cause of her last name."

"Very nice." Dr. Loni applauded. "That was a very brave admission."

"Ehmagawd, I have a fan club! I have a fan club!" Dylan jumped to the ground and danced to the beat of her raging excitement.

"I have a crush on Griffin." Kristen shimmied beside her like Shakira. "How cool will it be to show up at a party with a mysterious pizza heir?"

"What did Derrington mean by re-gifting?" Claire asked, feeling like a stone statue. She could sense the excitement swirling around her insides, but she felt heavy, immovable.

"What did Cam mean by 'big issue with Massie'?" The alpha stomped her wet bare foot.

"Why didn't anyone talk about *me*?" Alicia whined. "You're not going to tell Skye, are you?"

The bell rang.

"Ehmagawd," they all shouted, and then hurried for the door.

"Hit the lights," Massie barked.

The room went dark.

"What are we gonna tell Myner?" Claire asked as Massie scrambled to lock the door behind her.

"Bad sushi," everyone answered at once.

"Fine." Claire accepted their lame excuse without question. Getting busted by her geography teacher was suddenly at the bottom of the list of things to freak out about. Abandoned moral high horses, a mysterious camp-tramp named Nikki, and re-gifted cinnamon hearts had shot straight to the top.

Not necessarily in that order.

"Sit!" Mr. Myner pointed at table number three with his cleft chin. Positioned between the swinging kitchen doors and the carving station, the dreaded table was plagued by an invisible cloud that still smelled like a mix of soapy metal spoons and rare roast beef, even though the Café had been closed for hours.

"Meat seats," Dylan coughed.

The girls fought to suppress their giggles as they sat.

"You're probably wondering why I'm making you serve your detention here, in the Café, and not in my classroom." Mr. Myner—aka the Brawny Paper Towel Guy—folded his muscular, too-tanned-for-April arms across his log-brown flannel button-down.

The Pretty Committee examined their cuticles.

"Well, for starters, I'm not sure you girls know where my classroom *is*." He towered above them like a giant redwood tree and stared straight into Massie's amber eyes.

She fired back dozens of invisible hate daggers, each one Gillette Venus sharp.

"And don't think I'm going to let you turn this detention into an opportunity to cram for your finals." The corners of his full, dark lips curled into a "Ha! Take that" smile.

Massie looked away, refusing to give the cocky Birken-stalker the satisfaction of seeing her asphyxiate on lemon-scented cow fumes.

It was the first time she had seen the Café empty. Usually she was holding court at table eighteen, all the way in the far corner by the windows. And this unfamiliar perspective—without the lively chatter or pop-hiss of opening soda cans—made her feel strangely vulnerable and out of place.

"Now." Mr. Myner sat on the edge of their table and crossed his thick log legs. "Who would like to explain why you missed today's soil sampling?"

The girls giggled at his choice of words.

"Anyone?"

"Bad sushi," they answered.

He folded his muscular arms across his chest and squinted in disbelief.

"I know it sounds *fishy*." Massie smirked. "But it's true."

"Well, you missed out on a lot this afternoon," he responded sternly, in a way that was meant to fill them with regret.

"My gardener can always fill me in," Alicia said, with the wide-eyed faux sincerity that teachers and parents always bought.

"Joke all you want, Miss Rivera, but if you continue to take Mother Nature for granted she—"

"Um, s'cuse me, but we so do nawt take her for granted," Dylan interrupted. "If we did, why would we pay extra for Sonya Dakar's *plant*-based moisturizers and toners?"

"Great." He rubbed his palms together like someone who

was rarin' to go. "Then you won't mind spending the next two hours *feeding* the earth, as a thank-you for all those expensive moisturizers and toners."

The girls stared at him blankly.

"Follow me." Mr. Myner stood.

"Kumbaya," Alicia sneezed as they followed him into the sterile kitchen.

The instant they entered the stainless-steel jungle, Massie reached for her purple-lensed Chloé sunglasses. "This place needs a shot of color, ay-sap."

"Point." Alicia lowered her bamboo-framed Calvin Klein glasses from the top of her head. "It's all white and metal-y. I feel like I'm trapped in a giant iPod."

Kristen, Dylan, and Claire snickered.

"Enough!" snapped Mr. Myner, the hum of the gigantic dishwashers forcing him to raise his voice above its usual groovy late-night-DJ purr. "Remove your sunglasses and feast your eyes on *this*."

He stopped in front of a long stainless-steel table that held five black plastic bins stuffed with rotting food scraps.

"Ew." Dylan scratched the side of her leg with the tip of a mocha-brown suede cowboy boot.

The rest of the girls tried to escape the fermenting-garbage smell by burying their noses inside their shirts and inhaling their perfumes.

"*Au contraire*, Miss Marvil." Mr. Myner reached into a small white cardboard box next to the bins and pulled out five hairnets. "What you are smelling is the cycle of life." He inhaled deeply. "Isn't it powerful?" He exhaled with a satisfied moan.

"Sure is." Claire's eyes watered.

"Please put on the nets and rubber gloves and join me behind these bins." Mr. Myner demonstrated by stuffing his wavy black hair inside the webbed cap. "Any questions so far?"

Massie raised her gloved hand. "Um, why do we *have* to wear these?" She tilted her net like a beret. "It's nawt like it matters if we get hair in the food. No one's gonna eat *this*." She turned away from the rank bin of eggshells, coffee grounds, banana peels, and vegetable scraps.

"The earth will be eating it, and trust me, she has no tolerance for your mousse, sprays, and fruit-scented gels." Mr. Myner pushed open the side door, letting in a gust of cold but refreshing air. "Behold, OCD's compost."

The Pretty Committee stared in shock at a roofless, outhouse-shaped structure surrounded by piles of mud.

"The workmen who renovated our cabana had to use one of those," Alicia announced, "because my mom didn't want them going *numero dos* in our house."

"There's no way I'm going in there." Dylan pulled off her gloves. "You can expel me again if you want."

"Relax." Mr. Myner snickered. "No one has to go in. It's a *compost*."

"Given." Dylan slowly put her gloves back on, her baffled expression making it obvious she had no clue what a compost was.

"Compost is one of nature's best mulches," Mr. Myner explained. "You can use it instead of fertilizer. All you have to do is dump the good stuff in and watch as bacteria, fungi, worms, and insects gather. What remains after these organisms break down the soil is a delicious earthy substance your garden will love."

The girls stared back at him, frozen in disbelief.

"Just separate out the bread, grease, dairy, and meat or fish parts, and toss the rest in the compost," he said with the kind of joy one usually reserves for announcing puppy births. "If I hear a single word from any of you, you'll all be back here tomorrow. And I hear the lunch special is Mexican fish stew." He slid a metal folding chair against the kitchen door to prop it open, but it immediately slammed shut, sending the chair careening across the Café like a stone from a slingshot. The girls burst out laughing.

"Begin!" Mr. Myner slid another chair in front of the door and this time sat down to hold it in place. "Not another sound." He pulled a small black notebook from the back pocket of his moss-green cords and began jotting down his thoughts with a red mini-golf pencil.

As Massie tossed a fish spine in the trash, her anger toward Mr. Myner quadrupled. Not so much because she was sorting cafeteria trash after school—she'd known the risk they were taking by skipping class—but because Mr. Myner had caught them before she'd had a chance to recap after ESP. And the need to discuss was eating away at her like worms in a compost.

"Finally!" Massie stepped onto her gravel driveway, slammed the door of the silver Range Rover, and wave-thanked her driver, Isaac, for the ride. The instant he drove off, she let out a major sigh of relief. "I officially lift the ban on all OL topics and declare them OL."

"Huh?" Claire crinkled her blond brows in confusion.

"All *off*-limit car discussion topics like ESP, compost detention, and the bomb shelter are now *on*-limit discussion topics because Isaac is gone," Alicia explained, trying to wave away the rotten-trash smell that had glommed onto them like LBRs at a school dance. "Ew. I need a loofah."

"I need shampoo." Dylan pulled an eggshell out of her matted red hair and booger-flicked it onto the ground.

"I need a skin graft." Kristen examined her mud-stained hands.

"Well, what are we waiting for, ladies?" Massie linked elbows with Alicia and Dylan. Dylan linked with Kristen. And Kristen linked with Claire. "To the spa!"

Like a human Frank Gehry torque-chain bracelet, they marched across the perfectly manicured lawn of the Block estate, toward the rustic horse-shed-turned-sanctuary. Along the way, Massie organized her thoughts into discussion topics, so they could get down to business the instant they got inside.

1) Force Kristen to choose a date (Griffin?).
2) Force Alicia to choose a date (Josh?).
3) Force Dylan to choose a date (Kemp vs. Plovert).
4) Help Claire get over the re-gifting thing so she can ask Cam.
5) Discuss: What could Derrington's issue with me possibly be? Is he intimidated? Does he feel like he's not good enough? Am I too perfect? Is it alpha to ask him to the party anyway, or should I find a new date? WWSD? (What Would Skye Do?)
6) Ways to make Chris Abeley get over ex, Fawn. Example: Spread vicious rumor about her unbreakable bedwetting habit.
7) Ways to make Chris Abeley like Skye. Example: Give her a crash course in horseback riding.
8) Ways to make Chris Abeley *call* Skye. Example: Break into his cell phone and change all his stored numbers to Skye's.
9) Ask Alicia if there was a Hard Candy Galaxy Glitter eyeliner pencil in the bomb shelter. If not, buy one before the party.
10) Has anyone even *thought* about studying for finals yet?

The closer they got to the horse shed, the more Massie's

heart pounded with excitement. She needed some unobstructed alone time with her girls almost as much as she needed a Dead Sea–salt scrub. Fortunately, she was minutes away from both.

"Clll-aire!" a distant girl's voice shouted.

The Pretty Committee stopped at once.

"Clll-aire!" they heard again.

Everyone turned left, toward the quaint stone guest-house where Claire's family had been living for the past eight months.

"Layne?" Claire sounded surprised when she saw her friend speed-walking toward them. A clear backpack hung over the front of her torso, revealing a Chococat pencil case, a mini can of V8, a math textbook, an orange Lucite clipboard covered in old Transformer stickers, a blue Nokia phone, and several Slim Jim wrappers. "What are you doing here?"

Claire looked at the Pretty Committee apologetically.

"We're supposed to study for the math final, remember?" Layne tapped her backpack with a neon-orange fingernail. "I've been counting the ants on your porch for over an hour. At one point there were forty-seven."

Claire turned red. "Oh, no. I totally forgot."

"Gee, thanks." Layne eyed the Pretty Committee, silently blaming them for her friend's insensitivity.

"I mean, I didn't *forget* forget. It's just that I had deten—"

"Don't tell!" Massie coughed, reminding Claire that reveal-ing *anything* about the bomb shelter could cost them ESP and, ultimately, their future as eighth-grade alpha-boy experts.

"I . . . I had a dentist appointment and—"

"Whatever." Layne shrugged it off, like she did most things. "Let's just go now." She folded her arms across her backpack, bracing herself against the cool evening wind.

"Um . . ."

"She can't." Massie placed a composty hand on her J Brand denim–covered hip. "Because we're, um—"

"We're going to the spa," Alicia bragged.

"Perfect." Layne pivoted on the heel of her lime-green Converse sneaker.

Massie shot Alicia a thanks-a-lot glare. Kristen and Dylan snickered.

"Sorry," Alicia mouthed.

Claire looked at Massie, her blue eyes wide and shifting, like those of a baby seal caught in a trap.

"Layne," Massie asked sweetly, "are you made of Saran Wrap?"

"No."

"Then why are you acting all clingy?"

The girls burst out laughing, and Massie resumed her trek toward the spa.

She could hear the footsteps of the Pretty Committee in the grass as they followed closely behind her.

"You *owe* me," Layne called after her.

"I owe you *what*?" Massie practically roared.

Layne hurried to catch up.

"When I gave you the key to Skye's secret room, you told me I could come to one of your sleepovers every month."

Massie stopped and glared at her. The others stopped too.

"And?"

"And I'd rather go to the spa instead." She pulled out one of her three side-braids and re-braided it.

The Pretty Committee let out a collective gasp.

"It's nonnegotiable," Alicia snapped.

"What if I—?"

"Nonnegotiable," Dylan insisted.

Claire squinted toward the horizon. The sun was sinking, like it didn't want anything to do with this discussion either.

"What if I promise not to go to your sleepover next month, either?"

"Nonnegotiable," Alicia reiterated, only this time she said it to Massie, silently asking her for backup.

"Please—it's not like I'm Maksim Myaskovskiy," Layne pleaded.

"Who's *that*?" Claire laughed.

"Hilary Duff's stalker," she giggle-explained.

The Pretty Committee burst out laughing.

"Ugh!" Massie took the last remaining steps to the wood spa and gripped the massive barn door.

"Why do you want to go to the spa so badly?" Kristen asked, instinctively helping her friend slide the heavy wood panel.

"Because my brother, Chris, won't be here for another hour, and I don't want to sit outside in the cold anymore. Besides, it's getting dark."

Massie didn't say a word. Instead she tapped her chin and squinted, rolling this new information around in her mind.

"Massie!" Dylan squealed. "I thought you wanted to talk about—"

"Fine."

"Fine, what?" Layne asked.

"Fine, you can come."

"Huh?" everyone asked, including Layne.

"Really?" Layne gave Claire's wrist a triumphant squeeze.

"Really."

Claire grinned.

"Wait!" Alicia sounded shocked. "Why is this okay?"

"Does everyone have their cell phones?" Massie asked, her mind racing.

The Pretty Committee nodded.

"Then she can come."

The girls entered the warm spa in silence. Massie could tell by their not-so-subtle side glances that they had no clue why she'd accepted Layne's offer. But they would.

Eventually.

After a therapeutic multi-jet shower with plant-essence-infused water and five different body scrubs, Claire twisted a thick white towel around her clean hair and slipped on a disposable swimsuit—a gift to all spa guests, compliments of the Blocks.

The black one-piece sagged at the chest and gaped around her butt, but Claire was too distraught to care. Her crush had turned out to be a re-gifter and her best friend had obviously walked into some sort of trap. And no amount of cooling euca-lyptus creams or warming citrus oils would change that.

After sliding into a pair of yellow Havaianas, Claire flip-flopped her way across the white marble shower floor in the back section of the spa and pushed through the foggy double glass doors, leaving a floral-scented steam cloud of Decleor products behind.

The Pretty Committee, dressed in identical black bathing suits, were waist-deep in the emerald-green Jacuzzi, lounging behind a misty veil of chlorine and periodic blasts of Evian facial mist.

Layne lay barefoot on a white chaise lounge, dabbing her beading forehead with a piece of graph paper torn from her math notebook.

"Aren't you getting in?" Claire asked, dipping her toe in the hot, frothing water.

"I can't. I have my—"

"Ew!" Alicia covered her ears. "Don't say it *again*."

Layne sat up. "What word?" The corners of her mouth curled. "Peri—"

The Pretty Committee squealed, their horror echoing off the white tile walls.

"Why do you hate that word so much?" Layne teased with delight. "You're all gonna get it." She zeroed in on Alicia's chest. Her C-cups filled the bathing suit in ways Claire never would.

"I can't believe *you* don't have it already. I mean you're so developed and—"

"Layne! Opposite of go awn!" Alicia pulled her robe into the hot tub and covered herself. The Pretty Committee cracked up as the heavy terry cloth ballooned, then sank to the bottom. "Will someone puh-lease tell me why she's here?"

Claire waited nervously for an answer.

None came.

Massie lowered her head into the water, wetting the ends of her hair so that they stuck to her back like a swatch of black velvet. Then she stood, gripped the silver handrail, and stepped out.

After drying her pruning hands with a plush white towel, Massie reached for her phone. Without a word of explanation, she passed the towel around to the Pretty Committee, who somehow knew exactly what to do with it.

Once their palms were dry, she distributed the remaining cells to their rightful owners. The girls held them high above the bubbling water, awaiting further instruction.

"How 'bout a little music?" Layne suggested, oblivious to the ritual unfolding before her.

"Play the CD that's in my Prada." Kristen chin-pointed to the black messenger bag in the corner. "You guys are gonna love it."

As soon as Layne turned to get it, the girls' phones vibrated.

MASSIE: K, U ASKING G?
KRISTEN: NEED 2 C ESP AGAIN 2 B SURE HE'S HART.

Massie rolled her eyes and typed.

MASSIE: PARTY IS DAYZ AWAY!!!!!
KRISTEN: 1 MORE TIME. I PROMISE.
MASSIE: D, WHAT ABOUT U?
DYLAN: SO MANY CHOICES.
MASSIE: PICK 1.
DYLAN: NEED ESP 1 MORE TIME 2.

Massie sighed loud enough to let Dylan know she was getting impatient. Dylan held her phone high and typed more.

DYLAN: THE WRONG CHOICE COULD B BAD 4 THE PC.

Massie must have known she was right, because she moved on.

Claire's stomach pretzel-twisted. Was she next? She knew Massie wanted her to ask Cam already, to encourage the others. But how could she, knowing he'd been lying to her?

Luckily, Massie's heart-stopping glare passed over Claire and landed on Alicia. She was about to press SEND when a song that sounded more like a man projectile vomiting heaved through the white Bose ceiling speakers.

"What is *that*?" Dylan plugged her ears with handfuls of wet red hair.

"It's the *Saw III* sound track," announced Kristen, as if death metal was something fabulous she'd just discovered, like a cure for blackheads or Britney Spears's rehab diary.

"Turn it awff." Massie threw a wooden back-scratcher at the speakers, obviously not caring if they smashed into Tic Tac–size pieces.

"You don't like it?" Kristen screamed above the guttural wails.

"If the feeling of getting fistfuls of hair ripped from your scalp were downloadable on iTunes, it would be the *Saw III* sound track," Massie snapped.

"Point." Alicia lifted her cell phone an inch higher. "What about the flute music that was playing when we walked in? Can't we hear that again?"

"That Enya stuff is so mainstream," Kristen insisted. "Wait until you hear the next track. It's called 'Eyes of the Insane.' The lyrics are—"

"When did you become so alt.com?" Massie asked.

"When she saw Griffin, the dark lord," Dylan answered for her.

The CD was ejected and the music stopped.

"Thank gawd!" Massie muttered under her breath.

"What happened?" Kristen stepped out of the Jacuzzi and padded over to the sleek stereo. She pushed the CD tray back in and hurried back into the warm hot tub.

Projectile-vomit sounds barfed from the speakers once again, and the girls giggle-moaned.

Then, seconds later, the CD self-ejected.

Claire side-glanced at Layne and half-smiled.

"Why does this keep happening?" Kristen pressed her hands against the wet tiles, pushed herself out of the tub, and tiptoe-jogged over to the stereo again.

"My Bose has good taste," Massie replied.

Claire laughed much louder and harder than the other girls, and Massie shot her a curious glare.

"Sorry," Claire said, but it came out sounding more like "reeeee."

Massie kept staring. And Claire kept laughing. Then Layne joined in, which cracked her up even more. Desperate to stop, Claire slid underwater, but the muffled roar of the jets scared her into resurfacing before she was completely cured.

"What is going awn?" Massie smacked the bubbling surface of the water.

"Yeah." Kristen slid back into the hot tub.

The CD started up once again.

And then it ejected.

"Show them," Claire urged her friend as she fought the twitching corners of her mouth.

"Show them what?" Layne snickered.

"Yeah, show us *what*?" Massie narrowed her amber eyes, silently threatening social homicide if Layne didn't comply.

"This." Layne reached behind the chaise and grabbed a tiny clump of copper wires. She held them out in front of her with pride.

"I just pulled something that looked like that out of my hairbrush this morning," Dylan joked.

Everyone giggled, except Massie, who refused to spend one more second on the outside of an inside joke. "What *are* those?"

Layne sat up and cleared her throat. "It's a cluster of thirty-eight conductors that I knotted, then threaded through a metal bobby pin. But the real magic happens once you attach the—"

"Yawwwwwn." Alicia stretched her wet arms and patted her mouth.

"Tell them what it *does*," Claire urged.

"It's a signal interceptor," gushed Layne. "I threw it together with a little help from the World Wide Web. It's like a remote control."

"So *you* ejected my CD?" Kristen asked.

Layne nodded with glee.

"Can you intercept this?" A burst of bubbles surfaced around Dylan's butt. "S'cuse me." She giggled.

"Nicely done." Massie nodded.

"Thanks." Dylan beamed.

"Nawt you." Massie giggled.

Everyone cracked up.

"I am very impressed with *Layne*." Massie applauded. The Pretty Committee, confused at first by her open display of LBR appreciation, eventually joined in.

Layne stood and bowed.

Claire's heart swelled with genuine happiness. Finally, her friends were accepting Layne. Her two groups were coming together. No more separate plans or hurt feelings or—

"Um, Layne . . ." Massie's voice rose above the applause.

Claire's heart instantly deflated.

Layne continued to bow and spin and curtsy for her fans.

"Layne!" Massie shouted.

Everyone stopped.

"Yeah," she smile-panted.

"You may want to use the bathroom."

"Huh?"

Massie cupped a hand over her mouth like she was about to whisper, yet spoke at full volume. "That thing you have that keeps you from going in hot tubs is making me see *red*, if you know what I mean."

"Nooooo!" Trying to catch a glimpse of her backside, Layne spun like a dog trying to chase its tail.

"Ew!" The girls gasped and covered their eyes, but for some reason, Claire couldn't keep from looking.

"I don't see any—"

Claire sympathy-blushed for Layne. Unable to face her, she lowered her eyes and focused on her puffy white waterlogged cuticles. It didn't matter whether Massie was telling the truth or not. Either way, Layne was doomed to days of embarrassing period jokes at her expense. Claire had fallen victim to that when she first moved to Westchester and accidentally sat in red paint.

"Trust me, it's there," Massie insisted. "Layne, there's a bathroom in the back past the showers. Take all the time you need."

"Thanks." Layne reached for her clear backpack and bolted toward the double glass doors. She was in such a hurry, she left her phone behind. Claire considered chasing after her, but something told her that if she left, she'd miss out on something big. So she opted to soak for a few more minutes. It wasn't like Layne needed her phone in there anyway.

"Thank gawd." Massie bolted out of the hot tub the moment Layne was gone. She wrapped herself in a plush white robe and flopped down on a chaise.

"Well, I'm done." Alicia squeezed the chlorinated water out of her hair and hurried for the open seat beside Massie.

"Me too," Dylan echoed.

"Same." Kristen lifted herself out of the hot tub.

Claire knew she was expected to follow.

Everyone wrapped themselves in robes and curled up on the chaise beside Massie, like a tangle of newborn gerbils.

"Finally, some alone time." Massie squirted a dollop of

Nexxus VitaTress hair-food supplement onto her palm, finger-distributed it evenly, and then passed the tube around.

"Why is she even here?" Alicia snarled.

"Seriously." Dylan rolled her bloodshot eyes.

Massie sighed, then rested her head against the back of the chair and gazed up at the ceiling like she was considering something that had been weighing heavily on her mind.

"Tell us." Kristen gently rested her hand on Massie's terry-cloaked shoulder. "What is it?"

Massie's amber eyes seemed to fill with sadness and something else Claire couldn't quite identify.

"I have some major gossip to tell you," Massie told them confidentially.

"How many points?" asked Alicia.

"One thousand."

They leaned forward in anticipation.

"I need to make it quick, because it won't take long for Layne to figure out I was lying about the whole per—"

"Ew!" Alicia covered her ears. "Don't say it."

"I *knew* you were making that up!" Dylan high-fived her. "Genius!"

Claire hated herself for thinking for a second that the PC would ever respect Layne. She hated herself more for not running into the bathroom to warn her, now that she knew the truth. But one thousand gossip points was major.

Massie glanced at the double doors to make sure Layne was still out of earshot. Then she leaned forward. "IletLayne-cometothespabecauseIneedherhelpwithsomething."

"So it's a *use*? Phew." Alicia wiped her brow. "I thought you were getting soft."

"What about the *gossip*?" Dylan pulled a handful of red hair out of her comb and stuffed it into the pocket of her robe.

"YouknowthatbigsecretmeetingIhadwithSkyelastweek?"

They nodded again.

"Well,sheaskedmetomakeChrisAbeleylikeher.Shewants himtobeherdatefortheparty.That'showIgotusintotheroomearly. ItoldherIwouldhelpherifshegavemethekey."

"And she said *yes*?" Kristen's narrow blue eyes were wide with disbelief. "Just like *that*?"

"Kinda." Massie crinkled her nose with dread.

"Whaddaya mean?" Alicia asked.

"ShesaidifIfailedhershewouldtakethekeyawayforgood."

Everyone gasped.

"But we get it back for eighth grade, right?" Alicia asked.

Massie shook her head slowly.

They gasped again, then exhaled sharply, accidentally blowing out the vanilla-lavender pillar candle beside them. A thin ribbon of black smoke curled toward the high wood rafters.

"Why didn't you tell us sooner?" This time Dylan dropped a clump of hair on the floor.

"Some things are alpha-to-alpha."

"But this affects all of us," Kristen insisted.

"I wanted you to focus on getting dates," Massie confessed. "That's your priority. Let me deal with this."

At that moment, Claire felt sorry for Massie. She was obviously stressing over the deal she'd struck with Skye and had been too full of pride to ask her BFFs for help. It made Claire wonder what other things alphas kept inside. And how alone those secrets must make them feel.

"That's why I'm telling you. And that's why Layne is here," Massie assured them. "I need her to help me get access to her brother and—"

Right then, Layne pushed through the double glass doors, and Massie instantly changed the subject.

"And that's why I switched to AT&T."

"I'm going to make the switch too." Alicia nodded enthusiastically.

"But you need Cingular for the iPhone," Kristen reminded them.

"Point." Alicia lifted a pruny finger.

Layne stood above their chaises and looked down, her arms folded across her chest like she knew they had been lying. But she didn't look hurt. In fact, she was smiling in a soft, confident way, like someone about to make the winning move in a long, heated game of chess. "I *heard* everything you said."

"That's fine." Massie shrugged off the accusation. "It's no secret that AT&T has a good nationwide calling plan. You should consider switching."

"No, I mean about my *brother*."

Claire smile-bit her bottom lip.

"And Skye," Layne finished.

Massie focused on the grumbling Jacuzzi jets to keep herself from fainting.

No one said a word.

"Don't you want to know how?"

They nodded slowly.

Slapping a clump of mousy brown hair to the left of her head, Layne revealed a tiny, putty-colored earpiece nestled in her ear.

"You're *deaf*?" Alicia gasped.

"Hearing impaired." Kristen was quick to correct her.

"How did you read our lips from the bathroom?" Dylan sounded amazed.

"I heard deaf people have better vision than nondeaf people," Alicia explained.

"Hearing *impaired*," Kristen insisted.

"I'm the opposite of deaf," Layne beamed. "I have superhuman hearing, thanks to my Spy Ear."

They stared at the peanut-shaped contraption.

"I knew Massie was lying about my pants, because I was lying about my per—"

Alicia held up her palm. "Don't say it!"

"So I activated my Spy Ear so I could hear what you were saying about me when I left."

"Where did you *get* that?" Massie asked with genuine interest.

"EBay," Layne replied. "But it only works with a Nokia phone, and Nokia doesn't use AT&T, so you're out of luck."

Claire giggled. She was constantly impressed with Layne,

who had the uncanny ability to not let the Pretty Committee get to her. It was like she was made of Teflon or something, and their words just slid right off of her.

"So what's your point?" asked Massie, skillfully managing to put Layne on the defensive.

"I want to help," Layne answered, helping herself to the tiny available corner of the girls' chaise.

"Huh?"

"I want to help you make Chris like Skye."

"Why?" Massie wiggled free from the others and jumped to her feet, causing the Pretty Committee to collapse like a heap of old, worn stuffed animals.

"Just to help."

"Why?" Her voice echoed against the misty white tiles.

"Because I want my brother to get over Fawn. He's been so depressed lately, and he never wants to hang out anymore."

"That's it? It's that simple?"

"It's that simple," Layne assured her. "Oh, but if you could throw in one of those disposable bathing suits, I'd appreciate it. I think it would look cute with my gauchos."

Massie placed her right hand on her waist, letting the left dangle at her side, Saks-mannequin-style. She rotated her torso five degrees and lifted her chin ever so slightly.

"Rate me," she murmured through a stiff smile.

Her cap-sleeved midnight-blue BCBG minidress complemented the gray tights and metallic-silver Frye motorcycle boots that had just arrived from ShopBop. And her hair, thanks to a dollop of straightening gel and an early-morning blowout by Jakkob, was practically reflective. Chanel No. 5 wafted from her pressure points, filling Layne's glow-in-the-dark bedroom with the crisp smell of spring, a necessary change from the oily bovine funk of Slim Jims.

"What do you mean, *rate* you?" Layne clamped her limp, light brown hair to the back of her head with a neon-pink banana clip. The Spencer's Gifts–type accessory seemed to fit right in with the collection of neon face masks, highlighter-colored lightbulbs, and fluorescent rugs that surrounded them.

"I *mean,* how do I *look*?" Massie huffed, longing for her girls. "Give me a number out of ten."

"It's kinda hard to see in the dark." Layne bounced off her luminous paint-splattered duvet cover and flicked on the lights.

"Ehmagawd, thank gawd," Massie mumbled. "I was start-ing to feel trapped in an episode of *The Simpsons*."

Layne, ignoring the dig, circled Massie, slowly tapping her lip. "Hmmmm."

"What?" Massie's heart quickened.

Were the boots too loud? Tights too drab? Mini too mini?

"I'd say you're aaaaaaaaah . . ." She made one more rota-tion. "Seven."

Massie gasped. "Sev-uhn?"

"Higher than you expected?" Layne tightened the gold sash on her multicolored satin kimono, a bathrobe she some-how thought appropriate to pair with black knee-high Steve Madden wedges.

"Nope," Massie lied. "It's exactly what I thought you'd say."

She longed for the Pretty Committee, who never gave her lower than an eight point five, but knew her decision to ban them from this mission had been the right one. It would have been impossible to have an effective heart-to-heart with Chris if her friends were there, watching, giggling, judging. Besides, what if he started crushing on Alicia instead of—

Massie deleted that sentence mid-thought. It was the only way she could keep *her* name from ending it. After all, this was about Chris and Skye. There would be plenty of opportunities for Chris to fall in love with her once the room belonged to the Pretty Committee. Besides, she needed this time to contemplate her true feelings for Derrington. As of late, his maturity and loyalty were in question. But to be fair, he was a HART, at least as far as seventh-graders went, and she didn't want to give him up until she was absolutely sure she wouldn't regret it.

"Wanna help me work on my karaoke glasses? They're almost done." Layne pulled a metal cookie sheet out from under her bed. An assortment of screws, wires, batteries, computer chips, and tweezers were spread out upon it. A pair of old-school black Ray-Ban Wayfarers lay in the center.

"All we have to do is build a Starscroll-size projector and attach it to one of the arms. If my theory is correct, the dark plastic will act like a screen, and the words of songs will scroll across it. Meaning, karaoke! Anywhere. Anytime. No wires, no bulky TV screens. No hassle." She bowed, anticipating applause.

"Is your brother home?"

Layne nodded yes, then lifted her head.

"It's time."

"What's your plan?" Layne asked, sliding the cookie sheet back under her bed.

"I figured a good pep talk and a fun afternoon with me would be enough to get him off his girl-fast."

"That's *it*?" Layne's narrow hazel eyes widened.

"Yeah. How hard can it be?"

"O-kay." Layne snickered in a don't-say-I-didn't-warn-you sort of way and then flicked off the lights. "Follow me."

Massie pinched her cheeks for a quick burst of color, then repositioned her glossy hair across her right eye. She knew it was slightly wrong to fuss over her looks when she was there to promote Skye. But she still had to hold Chris's attention. And that meant leaving Ugly Betty on ABC, where she belonged.

The upstairs hallway outside Chris's room smelled like Thanksgiving dinner—warm, tangy, and dusted with cinnamon. Oriental rugs cut the center of the mocha wood floor, while lofty totem poles and Egyptian sarcophagi occupied the corners. It was the kind of creepy, eclectic clutter one would expect to find in Lara Croft's basement, and the total opposite of Derrington's modern glass cube of a house—which reeked of Lemon Pledge and had a fragile-don't-touch vibe.

Massie decided she liked the feel of Chris's house better. It seemed more welcoming. Passionate. Alive. But still . . . Her heart pounded, and she would have traded her new red, white, and blue Juicy inflatable beach tote for a sip of chilled Evian.

"Code red!" Layne banged, paying no mind to the DO NOT DISTURB sign from the Marriott's Timber Lodge time-share in Lake Tahoe, California.

"What?" Chris called, his voice muffled.

"Um . . ." Layne looked at Massie, her hazel eyes flooded with panic. "Uh—"

"Tell him there's a special girl here to see him," Massie whisper-suggested.

"I can't do *that*," Layne whisper-shouted back. "What if he thinks its Fawn?"

"Then he'll open the door." Massie rolled her eyes, silently accusing Layne of being an amateur.

Layne inhaled deeply, then did as she was told.

Seconds later, Chris was standing in the doorway, feet bare, Diesel jeans ripped at the knees, and a worn gray Harvard sweatshirt hanging off his fit frame. His hair was a little top-heavy and in need of a trim, and he was squinting, like he had woken up and was adjusting to the light.

Even depressed-dressed, he was a nine.

"Oh," he said to his visitors, sounding disappointed. "Hey."

"Surprise!" Massie pushed past him, slamming the door in Layne's face.

"Hey, what gives?"

Massie flipped the lock, ignoring Layne's incessant banging.

"So, uh, how ya doing?" Massie asked, her voice suddenly forced and hollow, like it was coming from a bad actor in a school play.

"Been better." Chris picked his black electric guitar up off the floor and sat on the edge of his unmade bed. He didn't seem to wonder why she was there. Nor did he seem to care.

Unsure of where to stand now that they were alone, Massie stuck close to the door and leaned against his bare navy-blue wall. She slid her hands behind the small of her back and angled her face left, showing off her better side. "So, how funny was it running into you at Galwaugh?" she tried.

He fell back onto his bed. The light blue throw pillows shook from the sudden impact. Massie wondered how a girl named Fawn could turn such a hot prep-school rebel into such a sad sack. What powers did she have? What was her secret?

Massie wondered if she'd be that intoxicating after a few more visits to ESP. The mere thought of it motivated her to push harder.

"Remember that blond girl I was with?"

He plucked a few chords, which Massie took as a yes.

"Well, she's the best dancer in our entire school. Not to mention the prettiest girl in the eighth, soon to be ninth, grade." Massie paused. "She was pretty, don'tcha think?"

Chris bobbed his head. Was he was agreeing with her or simply feeling the music? It was impossible to tell.

"What was her name again?"

Breakthrough!

"Skye," Massie offered. "Her name is Skye Hamilton."

"That's right." He grinned. "I knew it was something like that."

"So you've been *thinking* about her?" Massie's blood pumped faster, like it did when she knew her dad was about to give in to one of her demands.

"I guess." He strummed.

Yes!

"What have you been thinking?" Chris looked up, dark blue eyes gripping her like a sapphire-colored force field. "I've been thinking she has one of those nature names."

"I know." Massie beamed. "Isn't it—"

"*Fawn* is a nature name." He lowered his head again and plucked B-minor.

"Oh." She scanned the ill-decorated room for something reflective so she could run a quick check on her appearance.

Maybe her long bangs had been finger-swept too far right. Or maybe her gloss had faded or her cheeks had dimmed. And maybe if she could swing a quick touch-up, things would go smoother.

But all she saw was a black Formica dresser lined with mini cologne bottles, a glass-topped desk covered in pencil sketches of the some long-haired girl with devil horns and blacked-out teeth, and an old Dell laptop. The far wall by the window was dotted with crooked snapshots of his boarding-school friends, pictures of Tricky, and a thin white shelf stocked with gold riding trophies and first-place ribbons. Not a single mirror in sight. Unless . . .

The maroon T-shirt Scotch-taped to an oval frame was definitely a mirror. It *had* to be. And Massie was desperate for a peek.

There had to be *some* explanation for his lack of interest in their conversation. After all, no guy as hawt as Chris Abeley could possibly be *this* depressed over a girl. *Could* he? Another excited tingle zipped through her body. After a year of ESP, she would never have to ask herself these ah-nnoying boy questions again—she would already know all the answers.

"Oh," Massie chirped with exaggerated curiosity. "What's under here?" She pinched the bottom of the shirt, cocked her head, and lifted it—

"Stop!" Chris cast his guitar aside, creating a hollow off-key twang when it met the wood floor.

Massie quickly released her grip. The shirt swung back into place.

"What *is* it?"

"A mirror." He raced over, making doubly sure the shirt was back in place. "Well, it *was*. I covered it."

"Why?"

"When I look at myself, I see—" His voice caught, then drifted.

"What?" Massie made extreme eye contact. Chris met her gaze and held it again. And just like that, her pupils begged for mercy. As if his hawtness exuded rays more damaging than the Caribbean sun. "Tell me what you see," she managed.

"*Her.* I see *her.*" He leaned forward and buried his face in his hands.

Massie sighed in a poor-little-thing sort of way and rested a hand on his curved spine.

Chris grinned, trying to force happiness that wouldn't come.

It became clear that his indifference to Massie went far beyond over-parted bangs and matte lips. He was a true romantic who was truly heartbroken. Which was both ah-dorable and ah-nnoying at the same time.

"Have you tried listening to music?" Massie suggested. "That always cheers me up. Sometimes the words can be very uplifting."

Chris shuffled to the other side of his room, resting his lacrosse-toned butt on the corner of his glass (IKEA?) desk. He folded his arms across his chest and mumbled, "Open the closet."

Massie took apprehensive steps toward the narrow white

door to the right of his bed. She placed her hand on the plastic, made-to-look-like-crystal knob, and then glanced back, letting Chris know she was about to turn it.

He shrugged in a knock-yourself-out sort of way.

So she did.

"Ehmagawd," she gasped. "You have so many A&F henleys in here. Why don't you wear them anymore? They're so ah-dorable." She ran her fingers along the spring-scented, Bounce-softened sleeves.

"They remind me of—"

Massie turned to face him. "Why? Did she buy them for you?"

Chris shook his head no. "But I wore them sometimes when we were hanging out."

"Oh." Massie tried her best to sound sympathetic. The truth was, if Chris's eyes weren't so navy and his hair wasn't so shaggy and his teeth weren't so white, she might have used the tough-love approach. A get-over-it speech followed by a snap-out-of-it slap. But his magnetic hawtness made doing anything but staring impossible.

"What does your closet have to do with music?"

"Look closer."

"Oh."

Surrounding the henleys, below the shelf crowded with a weathered lacrosse stick, beat-up cleats, old comics, and obsolete Game Boys, the inside walls were covered in music lyrics. They had been written in red marker, mostly on a sloping diagonal, in thin all-caps.

ON MY KNEES I'LL ASK,
LAST CHANCE FOR ONE LAST DANCE.
—NICKELBACK, "FAR AWAY"

HOW COULD WE QUIT SOMETHING
WE NEVER EVEN TRIED?
—NICK LACHEY, "I CAN'T HATE YOU ANYMORE"

SO DONE WITH WISHING SHE WAS STILL HERE.
—NE-YO, "SO SICK"

Massie turned away in horror.

"You should paint over those ay-sap. They're not healthy."

Chris half-laughed, like it finally registered that she was there.

"How 'bout something more positive, like, 'In letting you go, I'm loving myself.'"

She paused so her words of wisdom could penetrate. But Chris's head continued to hang.

"It's JoJo. 'Too Little Too Late.'"

"I *know* who it is." His smile faded. "That was *her* favorite song."

Massie felt a rush of heat flare up inside her entire body. How could she have been so stupid? But then again, how was she supposed to know Fawn was a JoJo fan?

All hawtness aside, it was time for the direct approach.

"Maybe if you found a new girlfriend, you'd forget all about—"

Chris lifted his eyes. "Have anyone in mind?" He grinned, suspecting she was referring to herself.

Massie blushed. "Um, how about someone like Skye Hamilton?" she answered, keeping her mission in mind.

"Skye Hamilton, huh?" He grinned suspiciously.

"Yeah, why not? Don't you think she's pretty?"

Massie held her breath, terrified of his response.

He shrugged.

She exhaled.

"Because I bet you could get her. In fact—"

Chris stuffed his hands in his jeans pockets and shuffled to his shelf of awards. "What kind of girl breaks up with a guy for spending time with his horse?" he mumbled.

Massie closed the closet door and hurried to his side.

"So that's *really* why she dumped you?" Massie thought of Brownie and felt a loving pinch behind her eyes. "That *is* pretty evil." She paused to swallow back her emotions. "But Skye ah-dores horses. She would *never* do that to you."

"Why are you so into helping me?"

"Um . . ." Massie felt her heart beat in her ears. "Because I live for horses. And, um, horses can sense when we're sad. Which means Tricky knows you're sad, and that makes her sad, and *that* makes *me* sad."

A smile slowly spread across his face.

Massie giggled shyly and took a small step back.

"You really love animals, don't you?"

She grin-nodded.

He stared.

She lowered her amber eyes.

He continued staring. "Did you know that there are more than three hundred different breeds of horses and ponies on the planet?"

"Yup." Massie took a step closer. "And there are seven hundred and fifty million horses in the world. I read an article in *Teen Vogue* last year about a horseback-riding camp for handicapped kids."

"Yeah?" He nodded, encouraging her to continue.

"*No.*" Massie twirled the Tiffany diamond stud in her ear. "That's the point."

He raised his left eyebrow in playful confusion.

"I *never* read human-interest news stories in magazines. I go straight to the horoscopes, read the beauty and fashion tips, then look at the pictures." Massie said with pride. "That's how much I ah-dore horses."

Chris placed his hands on her shoulders and looked straight at her. "I would have read it too."

Was Chris hitting on her? Was she hitting back? What if he lip-kissed her? What if he didn't? What about Derrington? And *Skye*? Massie's hard drive was about to crash. There were so many questions and not nearly enough answers. Rarely was there a situation she didn't know how to handle. But without the wisdom of ESP, hawt boys were to her like Kryptonite was to Superman.

"Um, lemme see your ribbons." She quickly forced herself out from under his electrifying grip and moved closer to the highly decorated shelf.

"So we'll both be at riding camp," Chris said, his breath warm against the back of her neck.

"Yup." Massie pretended she was too mesmerized by his first-place gold cup to give the summer, or his soapy cologne, much thought. Romantic sunrise rides to Hunter Lake, trail-racing before lunch, and twilight grooming sessions with Tricky and Brownie were suddenly all Massie could think about. That, and Skye threatening to take away the room.

It was crucial she find the willpower to put her renewed mini-crush on pause, at least until Skye's party was over and the key to the bomb shelter was securely fastened to her Coach chain.

"So." Chris inched up beside her. He was starting to look like his old mischievous self again. His color was back, his eyes sparkled, and his movements were lively, like he'd spontaneously recovered from the flu.

"Did you hear about the wave pool they're building on the roof of Briarwood?"

"Yeah." Massie lifted his gold first-place hurdles award and examined it like a jewelry appraiser.

"Well, they start filling it on Wednesday. After school."

"Really." She placed the gold statue of the jumping horse back on the shelf.

"Yeah." He paused. "They're having a whole dedication ceremony."

"Cool." She touched his blue grooming ribbon. It was just as silky as hers.

"And if you're gonna be there, maybe we can hang out," he added.

Massie let the ribbon fall from her fingers. "Um, of course I'll be there."

And she would.

For Skye. For the room. For the future of the Pretty Committee.

For anything but Chris.

CURRENT STATE OF THE UNION	
IN	**OUT**
Asking Layne for help	DIY
Considering Chris	Doubting Derrington
Match faking	Match making

"Will you puh-*lease* stop looking over your shoulder?" Massie unlocked the door to the bomb shelter. "You're making me paranoid."

"You *should* be paranoid." Kristen shoved everyone through the dark doorway as if fighting her way into a crowded subway car. "If Mr. Myner catches us again—"

"If he catches us again, we'll have to dump more compost." Claire flicked on the industrial light switch by the floor. "Big deal. It's worth it."

"Point." Alicia lifted her finger.

"S'cuse me?" Kristen squinted. "Aren't you the one who said this was *wrong*?"

Claire blushed at the memory of herself preaching morality to the Pretty Committee. She knew her change of heart must come off as hypocritical. But that was *before* she knew Cam was keeping secrets. And if he could be immoral, so could she. Besides, at this point it was a matter of health. Thoughts of him lip-sharing gummies on a sunlit swim dock with Nikki or cloaking her in his beat-up leather jacket by the warm light of a crackling bonfire were keeping her up at night. In class, she was either dozing off or conjuring up more stomach-churning images of *her* Cam with a hotter, smarter, funnier camp crush.

He was betraying her and making her look like a fool in front of his friends and *hers*, and the only way Claire knew how to even the score and uncover the truth was to betray him back.

Stepping over the DIY scraps of denim and rhinestones left behind by the DSL Daters, Claire quickly settled into a pink faux-fur director's chair. She glared at the black monitor and willed it to go easy on her.

"Jalapeño and cheese, anyone?" Dylan grabbed a handful of popcorn from the movie-theater-style machine and dropped it in the hard-butterscotch-flavored snack bag. "Or should we go for something a little less Tex-Mex and more tropical, like, say, pineapple-coconut?"

"Ew." Alicia casually slid a bottle of pink Hard Candy Pussy Cat polish in the side pocket of her sleeveless black Foley + Corinna corset dress. "Are you *trying* to blow up before bikini season?"

"My guys like a little junk in the trunk," Dylan gleefully insisted while seasoning her popcorn. "And who am I to deny them?"

Alicia turned away from Dylan in mild disgust. "Hurry, Mass! What if one of the guys is confessing his love for me and we're missing it?"

"*Desperate* much?" Kristen passed out a steaming round of freshly brewed Starbucks nonfat vanilla lattes.

"Puh-lease! *You're* calling *me* desperate?" Alicia smoothed the stiff white collar that was peeking out the top of her sleeveless corset dress. "You're the one wearing a black T-shirt with a skull on it."

"And black nail polish," Dylan added, taking a seat.

Alicia grinned. "Did your mom see your outfit this morning?"

Kristen shook her head no. "I wore gloves and a white cardigan to breakfast."

"Did you have *deviled* eggs?" giggled Massie.

The girls cracked up.

"Did you eat them with a pitchfork?" asked Alicia as she climbed into her faux-fur chair. "Were they *sinfully* good?"

"Did you Grif-*fin-ish* them?" Dylan busted out.

Everyone doubled over laughing, except Claire, who was fixated on the monitor, waiting patiently for it to power up and put her mind at ease.

"This has nuh-thing to do with Griffin," snapped Kristen as she sat. "I've always had a dark side."

"Yeah," Massie snickered. "Your roots!"

Kristen rolled her eyes and blew on her latte.

All of a sudden, the monitor hummed to life. A rush of sweat pooled under Claire's underarms, releasing a sudden whiff of ocean-breeze-scented Sure.

A black-and-white shot of the classroom filled the screen. "We're in!" announced Massie.

The Share Bear must have been hibernating on Dr. Loni's desk, because all of the boys were visible in the horseshoe configuration of their seats, each one hunched over a composition journal, writing.

"Remember," Massie announced, "no one leaves until they pick a date for Skye's party." The bell sleeves on her purple-

and-white-knit Missoni dress brushed against her cuticles, which she had been nervously picking at all day.

Everyone leaned toward the screen, showing their eagerness to cooperate.

"Pens down," Dr. Loni's voice instructed from somewhere in the distance.

The girls leaned forward even more.

"I asked each of you to draw a map of your heart," Dr. Loni continued. "And now, I'd like you to share those maps."

The grilled-cheese-and-tomato sandwich Claire had for lunch started retracing its steps. Heartbreak barf was inevitable unless Cam somehow managed to prove that Nikki was his long-lost sister and "re-gifting" was code for "I love Claire."

"Griffin, why don't we start with you?" Dr. Loni walked the Share Bear to the seat by the window. A shaky image of a pale-skinned boy with spiked black hair, tight gray jeans, leather wrist cuffs, and a T-shirt with a 3-D rubber gargoyle clawing its way through the cotton rocked on-screen. He reached out and grabbed the Share Bear, fixing the shot on his sharp chin and full lips.

"Um, okay." His voice was gravelly and low. "The four chambers of my heart are dedicated to: One, taking over the family business . . ."

Massie high-fived Kristen, who squealed with delight.

"Two, the pursuit of knowledge."

"Ehmagawd!" Kristen air-clapped. "I *love* knowledge."

"Three, Hades, my pet ferret."

Kristen waved that one away like Celine Dion perfume.

"And the fourth chamber of my heart is dedicated to"—he reached below his desk and lifted out a worn paperback—"reading."

"Ehmagawd!" everyone shrieked, except Claire, who couldn't help feeling slightly jealous that everything with Kristen's crush was going so perfectly.

"It's like I invented him on *The Sims*." Kristen fanned her flushed face.

"And what *are* you reading, might I ask?" twanged Dr. Loni.

"Good question." Kristen ran her fingers along one of the bumpy pink crossbones on her shirt in anticipation.

"I bet it's a manual on how to skin a puppy," Dylan said.

"Ew." Alicia giggle-winced.

"A little respect for Kristen's crush, please," Massie insisted.

It was totally not like her to defend a guy in skinny jeans, but his family owned a pizza empire, and Kristen seemed willing to make him her date, so it all made perfect sense.

"The *book*, Griffin," Dr. Loni repeated with a little more emphasis.

Griffin lowered it. "You'll laugh."

"Wrong." Dr. Loni clapped once for emphasis. "We're inside the fortress of trust, remember?"

He surveyed the room. "Fine." He exhaled. "It's *The Notebook*, by Nicholas Sparks."

Surprisingly, not one boy laughed.

"Ehmagawd, I loved that book!" Kristen gushed. "I bawled when I finished it. B-A-W-L-E-D, wept!"

"Yeah, but you're a *girl*." Dylan snickered.

Massie elbowed her in the ribs. "I think it's sweet."

"Do you want to tell us *why* this book speaks to you?" Dr. Loni pushed.

"Why wouldn't it?" Griffin sounded defensive. "It's a time-honored romance about love lost and found again."

Claire listened for the inevitable snickers and jabs, but the boys were curiously silent.

Dr. Loni applauded. "Now we're getting somewhere." He paused and then lowered his voice. "Are you interested in continuing this journey, Griffin?"

"Say yes!" Kristen shouted like an overenthusiastic audience member on *The Price Is Right*.

"Continue!" Massie hollered.

"Do it!" Dylan bit off a chunk of her butterscotch-flavored popcorn bag.

Alicia and Claire giggled.

"Sure." Griffin half-smiled. "I'll continue."

"Yes!" The girls cheer-clapped.

"Good." Dr. Loni walked in front of the Share Bear. His portly torso filled the screen. All anyone could see was a big belly zipped inside a bright sweat-jacket.

"Move!" Kristen shouted, frantically waving her arms as if trying to clear a giant smoke cloud. But he didn't. And the bear, which must have been on Griffin's desk, facing forward, remained focused on Dr. Loni and his carb-locker.

"Now, son, why do you suppose a sensitive, kindhearted young man like yourself would want the world to think he's an angry, aggressive member of the underworld?" He placed his fingertips together in prayer position.

A noisy jackhammer, obviously blasting its way through concrete, bleated through the room before Griffin could answer.

"Dang that wave pool," snapped Dr. Loni. "I don't see why they have to work on it during school hours! Those machines sound so hateful." Once the short bursts stopped, he cleared his throat, then adjusted his tone. "Continue."

"Maybe the way I dress is a mask." Griffin tugged the bottom of his monster T-shirt. "You know, a way for me to hide my true self from the world so I can't get hurt."

"Awwwww," cooed the girls.

"*Breakthrough!*" shouted Dr. Loni.

The boys clapped supportively.

"I can't believe they're not laughing at him!" Dylan blurted.

"Why would they?" Kristen rushed to Griffin's defense.

"Well, it's just that he sounds so . . . *sensitive*."

"Sensitive is nice," Claire mumbled to her puffy red cuticles, even though she also thought the absence of heckling was odd for a group of boys.

"He sounds perfect to me," Massie insisted, clearly hoping Dylan's comment wouldn't change Kristen's mind, since she was the only was who was certain about her HART.

"Don't worry." Kristen leaned across Claire, placing a reassuring hand on her arm. "I'm all over him like tears on tissue."

"Thank gawd." Massie tapped a note into her PalmPilot.

"Congratulations, Griffin. How about you pass the Bear to Mr. Plovert."

The camera wobbled again. It finally stopped moving and focused on Chris's YOU LOOKED BETTER ON MYSPACE tee.

Dylan unwrapped a sour-apple-flavored Blow Pop and stuck it in her mouth. "Do you think he'll talk about me again?"

No one bothered to answer.

"The four chambers in my heart are dedicated to my white beagle, Wingman; soccer; Kemp's *Playboy* subscription; and—"

"Ew," Dylan practically spat while the boys laughed.

"And my fourth chamber is for girls who don't ask me what's wrong all the time."

The boys whooped and applauded in agreement.

"It's so true," bellowed a crackly voice from across the room. "Why do they do that?"

"It's like they think we're thinking something when we're not," Plovert continued. "When I'm quiet, it's 'cause I'm relaxed. I'm not thinking *anything*. But when *they're* quiet, they're really thinking things."

"True again!" the crackly voice chimed in again. "It's like the opposite. Girls think we're thinking things when we're not, and we think they're *not* thinking things when they *are*."

"It's all about open communication," Dr. Loni interjected.

"I also like cool girls," Plovert added.

"Hey." Kemp punched Chris on the arm. "I was going to say *that*. You copied!"

"Define *cool*," said Dr. Loni, ignoring the interruption.

"Girls who act like guys but *look* like girls. You know—they eat in public and laugh at dirty jokes instead of acting all grossed out by them."

"That's five chambers, Mr. Plovert, I only asked for four."

"Ha!" Kemp punched Plovert again.

"Yay!" Dylan waved her Blow Pop like a lasso. "Yay. Yay! Double yay!"

"They *can't* be serious." Alicia shook her head in disbelief. "Anyway, how do you know they're even talking about *you*?"

"Because I'm the only girl at OCD who's ever eaten in front of them."

Alicia lifted her "point" finger.

"So." Massie taped the PalmPilot stylus against her knee. "Which guy are you gonna pick?"

"I can't decide." Dylan knocked the green Blow Pop against her teeth while giving it some thought. "They're both HARTs."

Alicia rolled her big brown eyes.

"I liked her first." Plovert smacked his desk.

"I did!" Kemp smacked his.

"Gentlemen, it's time to translate your rage into words." Dr. Loni's voice was soothing. "You can have feelings for the same girl. It's very common. In fact, it can bring you closer if you let it. We'll be focusing on that next week."

"*J'adore* Dr. Loni!" Dylan blew the screen a kiss. "He's pretty much saying I should invite them both. And he's right. Two dates is so much more suitable than one! It's suitable times two. Su-two-ble! Ehmagawd, wait until Skye and the wannabes hear about this!"

"What famous couple will you dress up as?" Kristen asked.

Dylan glanced up at the black ceiling. "I know." Her soft red curls bounced as she lowered her head. "I'll be Demi Moore, Plovert can be Bruce Willis, and Kemp can be Ashton. You know, 'cause they all get along."

"Love that." Massie nodded approvingly at her PalmPilot. "So Kristen and Dylan have chosen." She smiled with some degree of relief. "We're making progress."

"When someone asks Dylan where Rumer, Scout, and Tallulah are, she can say she ate them," Alicia offered.

"Ehmagawd, Leesh." Dylan yanked the Blow Pop from her mouth. "If jealous was a number, you'd be infinity."

"And if conceited were bricks, you'd be the Great Wall of China." Alicia stuck out her tongue, a childish gesture that made them all crack up.

On screen, the bear was passed again. It stopped on the sleeve of a worn leather jacket.

Claire's stomach contracted. She would have known that sleeve anywhere. It was cold to the touch and smelled like sushi and Drakkar Noir.

"My four chambers are for rock music, my family, soccer, and—"

She closed her eyes. Held her breath. And vowed never to do anything immoral again if he would just say . . .

"Claire."

She exhaled. She had been wrong about Nikki the

camp tramp. From this moment on she would never doubt Cam—

"Liar!" Derrington fake-sneezed.

"What?" Claire gasped at the screen. "No. He. Is. Not!"

Several hands gently touched her back and rubbed it as if she were in labor.

"Liar," sneezed another boy.

"Liar!" sneezed another, until the whole class sounded like the nurse's waiting room on exam day.

"Calm down," insisted Dr. Loni, pronouncing the *l* in calm. "Why the accusations?"

"Maybe *he* should get a fifth chamber—for Nikki," said someone who sounded like Josh.

Claire covered her mouth to contain the heartbreak-barf. She hated Cam for making her look like such a fool. Hated him for having a mysterious summer girlfriend. And hated that she couldn't talk to him about it, because her source happened to be a secret camera in a bomb shelter.

"There's nothing going on with Nikki," Cam insisted, but like the boys, Claire had a hard time believing him. Was it the way he said "Nikki" that made her doubt him, soft and kind, as if he respected her? Or was it simply her name? Nikki. The way the two *k*'s stood side by side, like tall, thin BFFs, snickering and conspiring to steal her boyfriend.

"For weeks now you've been saying there's nothing going on with her," sighed Dr. Loni. "But then why does she send you gummy worms and cinnamon hearts? One of you is in denial? Which one is it? You or her?"

Claire couldn't believe it. Even Dr. Loni thought Cam was lying. How could she have been stupid enough to fall for his nice-guy act? Massie had once said that when a guy gave a girl a lot of gifts, he was hiding something. And Claire had shrugged it off, assuming she was jealous. Yeah, right—like Massie would *ever* be jealous of *her*. She should have known.

"Are you going to be honest with Claire and break up with her before camp?" Derrington asked.

"Stop!" Claire shouted at the screen. "I can't take it any-more!" Tears flooded her eyes faster than size zeros disappeared at a sample sale. She lowered her head into her hands and rocked back and forth.

"If you're so into honesty," Cam's tone hardened, "why don't you tell Massie the *thing* you don't like about her?"

Everyone gasped.

Massie stared at the monitor, grabbing clumps of pink faux fur from her seat cover. Her face was completely void of emotion.

"E-nuff!" Dr. Loni stomped his foot. "You're using each other's feelings as ammunition, and I won't have that. I want you both here after school journaling about your rage." He yanked the Share Bear from Cam and handed it to Josh Hotz.

"Hey, we're both wearing the same Polo button-down!" Alicia air-clapped. "I heart that."

"My chambers are for the New York Yankees, Ralph Lauren, soccer, and, unlike Kemp and Plovert, I like girls who act like girls, not dudes."

Alicia turned to Massie. "Done, done, and done. Sign me up."

"He makes his sister clean his room." Kristen sounded outraged. "Doesn't that bother you?"

"Why?" Alicia applied a coat of Hard Candy Lip Sorbet, as if Josh were on his way over. "I love when people do my chores."

"Fine." Kristen slid off her chair. "Alicia, Dylan, and I have chosen our dates. Now can we puh-lease get back to class?"

Alicia and Dylan stood.

"Go 'head," Massie said softly. "I'm gonna stay and watch a little more."

"Me too." Claire sighed, her heart broken into way more than four chambers.

The low, steady hum of wheels rolling over the Lyonses' hard-wood hallway floors rumbled like an earthquake. The sound got louder and louder, then stopped, right outside Claire's bedroom.

She had no fear. Her heart didn't race. And she had no desire to ask who—or what—was there. All Claire felt was numb. Whatever it was couldn't possibly fix her broken heart. And it certainly couldn't make her feel worse than she already did. Cam was a liar, Nikki was a boy-snatcher, and she seemed to be the fool. And until that changed, it didn't matter what was waiting for her on the other side of the door.

"Open up." Layne jiggled the bronze knob. "I can help."

Claire pulled her baby-blue comforter over her head and curled into the fetal position. She could see the outline of glittery stars through the blanket and wondered how the sappy design had ever made her happy, since, these days, happy was a concept more foreign to her than the Harajuku girls.

After some mild scraping and slight tinkering, the lock clicked and Todd, Claire's orange-haired younger brother, burst in, dragging a large, gray wheeled suitcase. "Where do you want it?" he asked Layne, who breezed in behind him and tossed her black straw cowboy hat on Claire's lemon-yellow CD locker.

Layne rolled down the turtleneck on her red wool poncho and surveyed the room. "There." She pointed to the brushed metal desk, stacked with binders, textbooks, and long thin pens that looked like yellow tulips.

Todd dragged the suitcase across the white throw rugs, leaving a wake of soiled sheepskin behind him. Once his mission was complete, he held out his hand and wiggled his fingers.

Layne slapped him with a half-eaten York Peppermint Patty.

"That's it?" he squealed. "That's my tip?"

"No, that's a *treat*." She lowered her face to meet his. "Your *tip* is: Join a sports team. Your arms are quite underdeveloped for a boy your age." Layne squeezed his thin, freckly bicep. "Now git!" She clapped twice and Todd scurried away.

"Nice pants, circus freak!" he shouted at the black-and-white polka-dot leggings Layne had tucked into fire-engine-red Converse high-tops.

"How do you do that?" Claire asked, her face the only thing that wasn't covered in blankets. "He *never* listens to me."

"I make things happen." Layne tapped her suitcase with pride. "Now get out of bed and come sit by the computer."

"What? Why? What are you doing here?"

"Claire, face it, okay? You've got hotline potential." Layne twirled the small gold dials on her luggage lock and yanked it open. "I sensed sadness in your font when we texted after school. So I came right over. I'm going up north to drama camp in a few weeks, and I need to know that you'll be okay without me."

The word *camp* conjured up another forklift-size heap of sadness behind Claire's belly button. Was Cam really planning to dump her for Nikki this summer?

"Now get out of bed and c'mere." Layne reached into her suitcase and pulled out a six-pack of Red Bull, a medium-size gold box of Godiva chocolates, a bag of pretzel rods, five Slim Jims, three loose slabs of watermelon-flavored Trident, and two large bottles of Smart Water. "We may be here all night, so I brought provisions."

Claire sat up. "How did you ride your bike with that thing?"

"I didn't." Layne unzipped the bag. "When I asked my mom for a ride to the Block estate, Chris offered to drive me."

"Really?" Claire asked, wondering if his recent encounter with Massie had anything to do with that.

"Swear." Layne crossed her heart. "Now come!"

Claire slipped into her pink Steve Madden slippers and shuffled toward her desk. "Wait. What do you mean we may be here all—"

"Let me start with a few questions." Layne pulled a mini mirrored clipboard out of her oatmeal-colored canvas Sunshine Tours bag. "How did you find out about Nikki?"

Sweat beaded across Claire's forehead. How could she have been so stupid? When she'd texted Layne about Cam and Nikki, she'd forgotten Layne wasn't supposed to know about ESP.

Layne tapped her silver-lead, teeth-mark-covered pencil against the black pad on her clipboard. "Waiting."

"Um, I . . ." Claire pushed back her yellow velvet Pottery Barn curtains and looked out the window down at the Blocks' kidney-shaped pool, which was shrouded in a baby-blue cover and coated with wet brown leaves. It was hard to imagine she'd be swimming in it in less than a month . . . and even harder to imagine staying afloat while Cam was at camp with—

"Wai-ting!"

"I read it in Cam's journal," Claire half-lied.

"You *read* his journal?" Layne slammed her clipboard on the desk. "Claire, I think that's illegal in this state!"

"It's not ill—"

Layne popped open a can of Red Bull. "When you snoop, you're bound to find something you don't like. And when you do, you can't confront the person, because you snooped. Do you think it's easy hanging out with Meena knowing she swiped my Rodgers and Hammerstein lyrics book and blamed it on *you*?"

"*What?*"

"Don't worry—I knew you were more the Andrew Lloyd Webber type, so I peeked at her journal and my suspicions were confirmed. And now I'm stuck in an anger cul-de-sac."

"Huh?"

"An anger cul-de-sac," Layne repeated, as if Claire were having trouble *hearing* the term, not understanding it. "All my rage can do is bike around in circles. It's a dead end. Why? Because I can't tell her I read her journal."

"You don't think I know this?" Claire's eyes filled with tears. She scurried toward the heap of T-shirt-covered throw pillows beneath her window and collapsed on them, face-down.

Seconds later, Layne was whacking her butt with them. Claire lifted her tear-soaked face.

"Want one?" Layne waved the Godiva box under Claire's nose.

"No thanks." She sniffled.

"Fine, then. Let's review what we know." Layne pulled Claire to her feet and dragged her toward the shiny silver desk. She reached for her mini mirrored clipboard and scanned the first page.

"I told you." Claire reluctantly rested her butt next to her Mac laptop. She could feel the cold hard slab of metal through her pink chenille robe. "He met Nikki at camp. She'll be there this summer. She sends him gummy bears. And cinnamon hearts, and then"—she sighed—"he gives them to me." Claire dabbed her leaking eyes with the sleeve of her robe. "All this time I thought he bought them and—"

"Well, I have to say I'm a little relieved." Layne spun in Claire's white padded chair.

"What?"

"Claire, all this time Cam seemed soooo . . ." Layne's narrow hazel eyes darted back and forth. *"Perrrfect."*

"He was," Claire said to her slippers.

"Yeah, but I mean perfect in that creepy way that serial killers are perfect."

"Huh?"

Layne exhaled, as if being the only person on the planet who truly understood life was an exhausting burden. "You know how serial killers act all nice and polite as a cover-up? Well, before we found out about *her*, I thought Cam was nice and polite. But now that I know he's not, I can stop thinking he's a serial killer. Get it?"

"I guess." Claire felt the quake of an impending smile. Somehow Layne always managed to cheer her up. Even on hotline days.

"May I?" Layne's index finger hovered above the POWER button on Claire's PowerBook.

Claire nodded yes.

While the computer whirred to life, Layne sucked back an entire Red Bull. She cracked her knuckles over the keyboard and went straight to Google.

"Let's find out who this mystery girl is, shall we?" She typed "Nikki" in the search bar.

Claire wrapped her arms around Layne's back. "You're the best!" She squeezed. A little factual information would calm her nerves. Without it, Nikki might as well have been a post–nose-job Ashlee Simpson look-alike who knew the words to Cam's favorite Strokes songs.

"One million, nine hundred and forty thousand."

Claire leaned over her shoulder. "Huh?"

"That's how many matches I got when I Googled her name." Layne clicked on the first one, called, "Next-Door Nikki." A pair of boobs bigger than J.Lo's butt filled the screen.

"Ew!" they giggle-screamed.

"Did you happen to get her last name?"

"Nuh-uh." Claire reached for a pretzel rod.

"How about the name of the camp? Did you get that?"

"It's something like Full Moon or Bright Moon." Claire rubbed her temples. "I can't remember."

They keypad clacked as Layne searched both of those names. "Nope."

"I know. Try MySpace. Maybe she has a profile."

"Genius!"

Claire sat on the metal arm of her chair to get a better view. Her teeth started chattering with anticipation.

"Good news." Layne leaned back, folding her arms behind her head. "There are one hundred and thirty-three thousand three hundred and thirty-eight Nikkis."

"How is that *good* news?" Claire snapped, unable to hide her frustration.

"On second thought, that *is* a lot to weed through, especially with finals coming up."

"Um, yeah!"

"I guess the best thing for you to do is avoid him." Layne gathered her provisions and started stuffing them in her suitcase.

"I can't." Claire's hands began to shake. "If I don't ask him to Skye's costume party, Massie will kill me."

"Well, there's *one* thing you could do." Layne rolled her suitcase toward the door.

"What?" Claire asked, hearing the hope and desperation in her own voice.

"You were the star of *Dial L for Loser,* right?"

"Yeah. So?"

"So? *Act!*" Layne insisted, reaching for the brass doorknob.

"Wait, where are you going?" Claire pushed herself to stand, ignoring a sudden wave of dizziness. Life had never felt so hopeless. "I thought we were going to pull an all-nighter."

"That's before I knew you snooped." Layne opened the door. "Snooping is a fool's game. A sucker's bet. Like I told you, a nonstop bike ride to the anger cul-de-sac."

"But I need to get out of the cul-de-sac." Claire desperately dashed toward her friend. "Help me."

"I feel your pain, believe me." Layne stepped back into the room and hugged Claire. The sudden affection made her eyes well up again. Was it possible to feel loved and abandoned all at the same time?

Layne released her and, with genuine kindness, wiped Claire's tears away with her thumb. "You think it's easy looking Meena in the eye, day in and day out, knowing she stole my songbook? But I do. I manage."

"How?"

"Take your mind off of it."

"How am I supposed to do *that*?"

"Try Sudoku." Layne blew Claire a kiss and placed it on her cheek before leaving her alone in her room. Alone with a broken heart, one hundred and thirty-three thousand three hundred and thirty-eight Nikkis, and no clue what to do next.

"If your initials are MB, freeze!" Skye's raspy voice sliced through the whisper-buzz of after-school gossip, the slamming of locker doors, and the thick flow of get-me-out-of-here traffic.

Massie, refusing to take orders from anyone regardless of her eighth-grade alphaness, slowed to a window-shopper's wander.

"We need to tawk." Skye hurried toward her, the decorative tiara on her head sloping toward her ear. Normally, if Skye had *needed* anything from Massie, and made it publicly known like that, it would have meant an instant social upgrade and an excuse for a celebratory Marc Jacobs bag. But Massie knew what Skye wanted. And it was nothing to get excited about.

"Over here." Skye tugged the bell sleeve of Massie's black cotton Paul & Joe mini polo dress, guiding her into the recessed corner by the water fountain.

The DSL Daters stopped by the shadow box filled with black-and-white photos of poorly coiffed alumni and watched from a distance, bodyguard style.

"Ah-lone!" Skye hissed to the Pretty Committee, who followed without hesitation.

"Why don't you wait in the Range Rover?" Massie asked,

137

making it clear with a pronounced brow lift that they had no choice. "Tell Isaac I'll be right out."

Claire, Dylan, and Kristen did what they were told, while Alicia lingered, probably to covet-stare at Skye's latest dancer-chic ensemble.

Turquoise leg warmers hugged the bottoms of her dark skinny AG jeans, while a wide-necked gray cashmere sweater slouched right, exposing a pale shoulder.

"Are those leg warmers from the Body Alive apparel store?"

"Yeah, but don't even bother trying to get them." Skye straightened her tiara. "When I take something from my parents' boutique, they're not allowed to sell it to anyone at OCD. Hamilton family rule."

Massie side-glanced at Alicia, knowing her friend was hardly the type to sit back while someone accused her of outfit theft . . . unless of course it was Skye Hamilton.

Alicia put a hand on her hip and stuck her face close to Skye's, but then thought better of it and quickly pivoted toward her friends.

"So, what's going on?" Massie asked; her tone drenched in innocence.

"*Nothing,*" Skye snapped. "*That's* the problem." She rambled on about trading the bomb shelter for Chris Abeley, and how she wasn't seeing results . . . which was totally unfair. It wasn't like Massie wasn't trying. And getting chastised by Skye in the crowded halls of OCD wasn't doing much to motivate her to try harder.

A chatty cluster of B-listers caught Massie's attention, and she felt a swell of anger build inside her as they passed. She resented the way they carelessly tossed their bags over their shoulders, the way they laughed, the way they grinned while thumbing the keypads on their cell phones. *Why couldn't her life be simple and fun like theirs?*

Instead, Derrington was telling a roomful of Briarwood boys that she wasn't perfect. She'd been coerced into playing cupid for OCD's eighth-grade alpha. The Pretty Committee was dateless for the most prestigious costume party of the year. And, worst of all, she could feel the bomb shelter slipping away from her manicured hands faster than a bar of L'Occitane lemon-verbena soap.

"So, is he into me or what?" Skye whispered, twirling a buttery blond curl around her index finger.

Massie smile-nodded, hoping Skye wouldn't pick up on her guilt. If the alpha ever found out about yesterday's unexpected Chris-visit to the Block estate, she would be done. No bomb shelter. No ESP. No hope. Even though Inez had been instructed to tell Chris she was out volunteering at the animal shelter, Massie would be known as a boy-snatching temptress.

But what was she supposed to do? Tell the *truth*?

"Um, well, here's the thing . . . I sent Chris away because I was wearing baggy weekend sweats and my hair was begging for a hot-oil treatment. And even though he's not my official crush, and Derrington *is*, I've been a little confused lately about who I like more, and just in case it turns out I'm into Chris and not Derrington, I didn't want him to see me on a night when I was rating below an eight. Make sense?"

Yeah, right!

"Well, is he?" Skye slid the gold locket across its chain, then popped it in her mouth.

"Is he what?" Massie stalled, trying to buy some time.

Skye spit out the locket. "Is Chris *into me*?"

"I'm *working* on it."

"Work harder. My party is only—"

Massie lifted her index finger. "Oh, hold on a sec."

She flipped open her not-really-ringing Motorola Razr, pushed a few buttons, and moved her eyes across the blank screen for a few seconds. "This just in . . ." She snapped her phone shut. "Chris will be at Briarwood's wave-pool dedication ceremony tomorrow after school. At first he didn't want to go, but I convinced him, thinking it would be a great place for you guys to"—she made air-quotes—"'run into' each other."

"Love that!" Skye expressed her joy with a quick arabesque.

"Told you I'd take care of it." Massie knotted the green-and-white silk Pucci scarf around her neck. "You just had to be patient."

"I knew I could trust you." Skye fished around the inside of her pink leather Coach hobo tote, probably searching for a token of her appreciation. Maybe a secret alpha ring or a special solid-gold copy of the room key.

"But just to be sure . . ." Her expression hardened. "Take

this." She handed Massie a digital watch with a cheap black plastic band, the kind sold near the cashier's counter at drug stores and that tech geeks wear with pride. The LED screen glowed blue and a bell icon flashed in the top left-hand corner.

"The alarm will go off at 7:30 p.m., Saturday night. If it rings and Chris isn't at my party, playing Brad to my Angie, you'll find your key to the bomb shelter at the bottom of the Hudson River."

Massie half-expected a flash of lightning or a *mwah-ha-ha* laugh to follow Skye's villainish threat. But the beautiful blonde simply stared back at her, blue eyes shimmering, her skin glowing, and her smile radiating.

Massie's midday latte began working its way back up her throat. "No problem." She dropped the watch into her mint-green Marc Jacobs Heidi bag, then forced a casual grin.

"Oh, and speaking of dates, do your friends have any yet?"

"Ehmagawd, do you always worry this much?" Massie shook her head in disbelief. "You poor thing."

"I'm nawt *worried*, I'm just—"

Massie promptly made her move down the now empty hall, toward OCD's main exit. "Try the hot-rocks massage at Retreat." She pushed through the glass doors. "If that doesn't get rid of your pre-party jitters, nothing will."

Before Skye had a chance to respond, Massie was gone.

Massie quickly scanned the rain-soaked parking lot. Hair-frizzing dampness must have forced everyone into their respective cars faster than usual. And with everyone gone, Massie had no trouble spotting her target.

"Abeley, wait!"

Layne stood in front of the open door of her mom's silver Lexus, nose in the air, searching for the person who'd beckoned her.

"Over here." Massie waved, ignoring Layne's gigantic gold glitter-covered sunglasses. Because when someone wears oversize gold glitter-covered sunglasses, they want to be acknowledged. And Massie refused to be manipulated twice in one day.

"Is Chris driving?" She tilted her head toward the Lexus.

Layne nodded yes. She was wearing a clear plastic rain poncho and knee-high, yellow-ducky-covered rubber boots.

"Switch with me," Massie demanded when she got closer.

"Operator?"

"Switch with me." Massie opened a tube of Candy Apple–flavored Glossip Girl and quickly applied some. "Chris needs my help. He's still depressed."

"But . . ." Layne glanced at the Blocks' Range Rover. The Pretty Committee was inside, noses pressed up against the windows, anxiously awaiting the details from the Skye confrontation.

"No buts." Massie stomped her foot. "I'm going with Chris, and you're going with the Pretty Committee."

Layne pursed her lips as if contemplating this offer—an offer any other girl in their grade would have paid for. "Is Claire in there?"

"Given."

"Does she get dropped off first or last?"

Massie rolled her eyes. "Last, ah-bviously. She lives where we park the car."

"Hmmmmmmm."

"Layne!"

"Fine, I'll do it." Layne pushed her glitter glasses over the slight bump on the bridge of her nose. "For Chris."

"Thanks." Massie hurried toward the Lexus before Layne had a chance to ask for something in return.

And then she stopped.

The sight of Chris's head poking over the top of the black driver's seat sent a paralyzing tingle through Massie's body. It originated behind the button on her denim mini and shot straight to the backs of her freshly shaved kneecaps. The natural wave in his thick hair was mussed to perfection, creating that accidental ah-dorableness products like Bed Head strive to capture.

She had about six seconds until she reached the Lexus. Six seconds to come up with a plan to cheer him up and make him forget about Fawn once and for all. A super-speedy problem-solving session was her only option. So she asked herself the following questions:

Q: What cures sadness?

A: A new leather handbag (Chloé, Marc Jacobs, YSL, Dior, Coach, Miu Miu, Prada).

Q: What cures rejection?

A: New flats or hard-to-find boots (Chloé, Marc Jacobs, YSL, Dior, Coach, Miu Miu, Prada, Tory Burch, Frye, Calypso).

Q: What cures depression?

A: A new haircut and color (see Jakkob).

Done!

A satisfied half-smile illuminated her face as she texted her fab hairstylist with the plan. He responded immediately. And then, like a guided missile, Massie headed straight for her target.

"Surprise!" she bellowed after yanking the door open.

"Hey, you're not my sister." Chris looked pleasantly alarmed.

She lowered herself daintily onto the black leather passenger seat and made a show of crossing her legs so he would notice her calf-high red motorcycle boots.

"Do what I say and you won't get hurt." Massie poked a tube of Hot Chocolate Glossip Girl in the side of his rib cage. He was wearing a navy henley under his dark Levi's jean jacket. Had he been hoping to run into her, or was his old stylish self coming back? Either way, it was good news.

"What have you done with Layne?" He turned the key and started the car, making it clear that it didn't really matter.

"She's fine." Massie put a little more pressure on the tube of lip gloss. "Now drive. And don't stop until you get to Forest and Main."

Chris backed out of the parking space and Massie searched for her favorite radio station, as if playing his copilot was something she did every day. Once she heard Justin Timberlake's latest single, she cranked up the volume, rolled down the window, and sang along, wishing the girls at OCD could see her now.

Fluffy clouds spread over the sky like cashmere lint balls on last year's winter-white sweater. The air smelled freshly washed from the earlier afternoon rain, and the tree-studded streets glistened like a fresh blowout. It felt like they were driving through a commercial for new beginnings.

"Wait!" Massie gripped the black leather hand rest. "You're in the ninth grade, right?"

"Uh-huh."

"Then how can you drive?"

"It's easy." He smiled softly, exposing an ah-dorable white fang at the side of his mouth. "I hit the gas when I want to go and brake when I want to stop. The rest of the time I pray I don't hit anyone."

"Aw-nestly?" Massie's heart revved.

"Yeah, why?" He turned to her, practically searing her lashes with his fiery blue eyes.

"Ummmm." Massie stalled while considering her next move. If she seemed afraid, he wouldn't think she was cool. If she seemed shocked, he wouldn't think she was cool. If she did anything other than high-five him for being such an outlaw, he wouldn't think she was cool.

"I love it!" She lifted her palm.

He lifted his.

They met and slapped. Electric currents shot up her arm.

He tilted his head back and cracked up. "You're cool for a girl."

"What's *that* supposed to mean?" She tried not to sound like she was shopping for compliments, even though she was.

"It means, when I told Fawn I drove illegally she practically jumped out of the car."

"Why would she do that?" Massie dug her nails into the bottom of her seat. "It seems like you know what you're doing."

"I do." He grinned.

"How?"

"I have my license."

Massie searched his face for an explanation. He revealed nothing.

"How?" She giggle-insisted.

"I was held back a year for causing trouble. That's why I got shipped off to boarding school in London." He side-glanced at her, then quickly turned his attention back to the road. "Satisfied?"

She felt herself smile. "You don't seem like a troublemaker."

"You don't seem like a kidnapper."

"You're funny," Massie accidentally giggle-blurted, then blushed. She turned to the window to hide her cheeks and focused on a blond skateboarder rumbling down the rain-slicked sidewalk. He looked a little like Derrington.

She thought about her supposed boyfriend—a goofy, makes-you-wanna-laugh-out-loud kind of guy—and suddenly wondered if she had been selling herself short. After all, Chris was clever, Abercrombie hot, a licensed driver, and all around more mature. Massie was about to ask herself which one made a more "suitable" crush for the eighth grade. But the answer was ah-bvious.

"Now will you please tell me where we're going?"

"Just drive."

He snickered.

"See, girls aren't so bad," she told him.

"You're not like most girls."

"Puh-lease. There are tons of girls like me out there," Massie lied.

"Yeah, maybe."

"Really?" she screeched. But she quickly remembered her mission: Skye . . . secure the room . . . ESP access . . . rule eighth grade . . . become boy expert . . . Massie forcibly put her ego aside. "You mean you think you can, you know, move on?"

He cupped her shoulder. "It's very possible." He squeezed.

A panic-bolt zipped through Massie's entire body. Could he sense her terror? Did he realize he was dealing with an inexperienced lip-kisser? Or was he too smitten to care? What about Derrington? And *Skye*?

Massie leaned toward the radio, giving Chris and his electromagnetic love-palm the slip. An invisible handprint, hot and alive, lingered on her back long after he returned his hand to the wheel.

"Let's have some fun!" She cranked up the volume.

Chris lowered his window.

They banged their heads to the final chorus of the Fray's "How to Save a Life" and kept on singing while the DJ announced the next block of songs. "But first"—he deepened his already deep voice—"here's a little blast from the past for all you fools in luvvvv."

They lowered their heads in preparation, and Massie couldn't help giggling into her A-cups. Doubling on Derrington's bike was so out.

Suddenly, a heartbroken pop star's nasally lament whined through the speakers.

JoJo.

Ohh, no.

Come with me, stay the night
You say the words but boy it don't feel right

Massie's insides froze. Her nervous system flashed code red. A C-list DJ was ruining her plan!

Now what? Kill the volume? Start screaming? Fake barf?

Without a word, Chris poked the LCD screen on the dash and pressed OFF. His expression was similar to Bean's when Massie left for school every morning—pitiful and forlorn. On one hand, his show of emotion was sweet. Derrington would never have the confidence to reveal his softer side. But on the other, it was disturbing. Chris was ah-bviously far from cured.

"What's wrong?"

"Nuthin'."

Massie immediately considered getting her jaw wired shut. How could she have been so stupid? According to ESP, guys *hated* that question.

He didn't make another sound until they arrived at Jakkob's salon.

"Here we are." Massie tried to sound upbeat. "Park right in front."

Chris pulled the key out of the ignition. "What are we doing at a hairdresser's?" he practically spat. The smoldering light behind his blue eyes was fading fast.

Massie hurried out of the car and opened the door to Jakkob's salon. "There is nothing, and I mean nuh-*thing*, a new haircut won't fix. Once you see your new look, you'll have the confidence to move on and hang out with new—"

"I'm not a chick." Chris sat firm, refusing to betray his manhood by leaving the car.

"Tell that to your hair," she tease-shouted, eyeing the cute, chestnut-colored wings poking out from the side of his head.

"That bad?"

Massie discreetly crossed her fingers. "Worse."

Chris lowered his head, stepped of the car, and followed her inside.

"Mahh-ssie." Jakkob padded across the black marble floor of his moody salon in gray Gucci loafers, spreading his arms wider with each step, making it clear he expected a big hug. His dark McDreamy hair had recently been dyed Donatella-blond, making his ice-blue eyes and dark airbrushed skin pop.

"Jah-kk." Massie shuffle-ran straight into his embrace.

His familiar smell—fruity conditioner, chemicals, and CK One—made her think of prepping for black-tie soirees, birthday parties, and any other event that called for a professional.

"Is that heem?" he muttered, his tightly trimmed goatee tickling her earlobe.

"Yup."

When they broke apart, Jakkob oversmiled at Chris.

"Hull-uh, I'm Jah-kkob." He extended a St. Tropez–tanned hand, which looked extra brown against the cuffs of his crisp lilac Thomas Pink button-down.

"Hey." Chris shook politely, even though his darting eyes made it obvious he was searching for a way out.

Regardless, Massie bubbled with pride. She'd gotten Chris there on a moment's notice and convinced Jakkob to clear his schedule. So they'd had a minor musical setback. Now that they were at the salon, everything was going to work out. A makeover would give Chris enough confidence to sweep Skye off her super-arched feet, and the Pretty Committee's social status would be locked like an LV steamer trunk at curbside check-in.

"Come." Jakkob put an arm around Chris and escorted him to the black marble styling station in the rear, where the only shot of color came from the bright red hair dryer hanging alongside the mirror. Massie trailed behind with delight.

"So, whaddaya say we make you ze best *you* poss-hible?" He raised the black velvet seat with a few pumps of his foot.

"Whatever." Chris shrugged, avoiding the stylist's eyes in the oval mirror.

Jakkob shot Massie a did-he-just-say-what-I-think-he-said look.

"What-*ever*?" Massie stood behind Chris, addressing his reflection. "Wrong answer."

Jakkob nodded in agreement as he swung a red cape over Chris's torso with the grace of a matador.

"What do you *want* me to say?"

Both Massie and Jakkob placed their hands on their hips, cocked their heads, and looked at him disapprovingly.

"What?"

"This cut is about so much more than a few highlights and a snip," Massie insisted.

"Highlights?" Chris's face turned seasick green. "I'm a *guy*!"

"She's right," Jakkob continued. "Etz about taking cuhntrol and making changez. And that meanz be-hing man enough to try zomething new. Even if your friendz aren't doing eet."

Massie's tone softened. "Chris, I think what he means is, in life there are passengers and there are drivers. Be the driver, Chris. BTD."

"Mmmm." Jakkob forced his hands through Chris's tangled dark hair. "You need to drive."

"Fine." He sighed. "I'll drive."

They spent the next thirty minutes sipping lattes from gold china mugs and leafing through celebrity hairstyle magazines. Finally, they all agreed that Zac Efron's cut and color would complement both Chris's bone structure and skin tone. And they were right.

Two hours later, the light behind Chris's eyes was illuminated once again, and his jawline looked sharp enough to file acrylics.

"I hate to braahhhg, but he looks incredi-bull," Jakkob said to his reflection while Chris was in the bathroom.

"You're a genius." Massie slapped her Visa in his palm.

"It's nice to zee you with han older boyfriend," Jakkob mused as he walked the plastic card to his Aguilera-blond receptionist. "Derrin-tun was cute, but this one zeems better for you. Moh ma-ture. And your children? Zoopa-models foh sure."

"He's nawt my boyfriend," Massie said unconvincingly. "I'm setting him up with a friend."

"S'cuse me?" Jakkob slapped his heart in shock. "Would you just *give* Alicia those fahntaztik red motorcycle boots of yoh-rz?"

Massie beamed. Leave it to Jakkob to notice her boots. "*Nev*-er."

Jakkob pursed his lips in a well-that's-exactly-what-you're-about-to-do-with-Chris-if-you-give-him-away sort of manner.

"It's a long story," Massie blurted, desperate for a subject change.

"Well, let's ope it az a appy ending." Jakkob oversmiled again as Chris joined their circle.

"Ah-greed." Massie snickered at the enormous understatement.

"Thanks again, man." Chris slapped Jakkob's bicep.

"Pleasure." He winked and then handed Massie her card.

Massie winked back and followed Chris back to the Lexus, considering Jakkob's advice. A hawt older guy with a driver's license wouldn't be the worst thing for her eighth-grade persona. It would be much more enviable than a perma-shorts-wearing soccer goalie.

Hmmmmm.

Shaking the dangerously impure thoughts from her head, Massie saved the "Derrington vs. Chris" file as a "draft," with plans to reopen it after Skye's party.

"So?" she asked once they were zooming down Main Street.

"So what?" Chris gripped the wheel tighter than he needed to.

"Do you love it or do you luhhh-ve it?"

"It's just a haircut."

Massie felt her heart collapse like a crumpled love letter.

"Too many people think making changes on the outside will help them on the inside. But that's not how life works." He paused. "At least not mine."

Massie shifted her body toward the window, wondering if the heavy sadness spreading inside of her was what LBRs often referred to as "failure"?

"Until now."

"Huh?"

"I said, that's not how my life worked until *now*." He smiled peacefully at the yellow traffic light ahead and gently stepped on the brake. "You're special, Massie."

She continued to face the window. Only this time she felt light and buoyant, like "failure" had just been painted yellow and filled with helium. And despite Derrington and Skye and the bomb shelter and ESP, she couldn't control her overwhelming need to return the compliment.

"I like your shirt."

"I like *you*."

They waited out the rest of the red light in awkward silence. Massie's thoughts collided in her brain like smelly rock boys in a mosh pit. Temptation smashed into Guilt which crashed into Insecurity and bashed into Loyalty. It was impossible to isolate a single one and reason with it. They were moving too quickly and with more force than she could possibly harness.

"You remind me of Tricky," Chris continued, once they were moving again.

Massie turned to him, her crinkled brows asking if that was a compliment or an insult.

"It's a compliment," he said, reading her mind. "You're both sensitive. You're both strong. And"—his navy eyes moved across her cheeks—"you're both really well proportioned."

Massie's burning cheeks betrayed her again. She lifted her mint-green bag to her face and rummaged among tubes of Glossip Girl, purple ink pens, her Motorola Razr, her PalmPilot, her iPod, a YSL key chain, a black quilted Chanel makeup bag, and a mini photo album of Bean and Brownie, pretending to search for something incredibly important.

But then she saw the pulses of flashing blue light thumping inside like an alien's heartbeat. It was the bell icon on Skye's cheap digital watch.

And she turned red again, this time out of frustration and rage. She had three days left to convince Chris that *Skye* was the horse, not her. A possibility he didn't seem the least bit open to.

Not that she blamed him.

"Clam diiiip," burped Dylan.

Kemp Hurley and Chris Plovert laughed so hard they practically shot sea-foam-flavored seltzer from their nostrils.

"Try to remember you're in public," Alicia hissed loudly,
probably hoping Josh Hotz might hear. But he was buried deep
within the sushi-popping crowd with Derrington and Cam,
dropping shrimp tails in women's open handbags, killing time
before the dedication ceremony.

The evening's guest of honor—an enormous empty wave
pool—spanned most of the roof atop Briarwood Academy's
main building. Any free spaces around its edges were filled
with anxious wannabe surfers, proud donors, and the women
who loved them. A clear plastic bubble overhead, the kind
Claire first saw over the courts at the Blocks' tennis club,
kept everyone warm, while playing into the fish-tank motif
the party planners seemed to be going for. Sexy mermaids
glided through the pearl-clad crowd, offering oysters, steamed
conch fritters, and lobster tails in low-fat butter sauce. And
a string quartet dressed as penguins promised the crowd a
night full of water-themed songs. "Octopus's Garden" by the
Beatles was the current selection.

"Lobster tail?" A redheaded mermaid in a green-glitter-covered spandex costume shoved her silver tray into the Pretty Committee's tight circle.

"No thanks!" Alicia shouted toward Josh, who was now just a few feet away, snickering into his shrimp-filled hands with Derrington and Cam. "No food for me."

Dylan pinched two lobster tails, baptized them in butter, and stuffed them both in her mouth. "What is invisible and smells like bananas?" She chewed, the tips of the tails slapping against her shiny lips.

The boys shrugged.

"Monkey farts!"

Kemp and Plovert cracked up. Massie, Alicia, and Kristen rolled their sparkle-dusted eyes in disgust.

Normally, Claire would have laughed along with the guys, but tonight she could barely fake a smile. Even her outfit— loose, faded Seven hand-me-downs and a plain red long-sleeved tee—said, "I'm too upset to care." And Cam, who was joking around with his friends, totally oblivious to her pain, was making things worse. How could he be so happy-go-lucky when the pit in her stomach was reaching wave-pool depths? Could he not sense her angst from the terse IM responses she had sent him the last few nights? Not knowing what else to do, she spite-turned her back to him.

"Tonight's the night," Massie whisper-insisted. Her gold anchor drop earrings swung with conviction. "You guys better ask your crushes to the party tonight or—"

All of a sudden, Skye threw her arms around Massie and Alicia with fake affection. "Here are my little Cheetah Girls."

The DSL Daters stood behind her, tittering. "I've been looking for you all night." She shimmered in the formfitting seaweed green sequined mini she'd worn to her spring dance recital. Her messy updo was randomly adorned with gleaming starfish and sea horse clips. "Are you all set with your dates?"

"Yup," Massie answered a little too quickly. "All set."

Alicia, Kristen, Dylan, and Claire nodded like bobble-heads.

Skye leaned in to Massie's ear. "Any updates on you-know-who?"

"It's all under control." She wink-nodded.

"Promise?" Skye rubbed the gold locket across her glossy mouth. "Because he'd be the perfect Brad, especially with that incredible new haircut. And everyone says I have lips like Angie's, so—"

"Sounds great," Massie managed.

"It will be. My costume is all set. I'm just missing one thing."

"Not for long." Massie beamed.

And just like that, Chris and his new Zac Efron hair managed to squeeze through the thickening crowd. He was wearing a crisp blue pair of Diesels, a brown henley, and a Levi's jean jacket. His confident swagger proved he knew how good he looked.

"Hey, you." Skye quickly ran her fingers through his highlights.

Claire couldn't help noticing her confidence and hoped that after a year of ESP access, she'd be just as bold.

"Hey, Skye." Chris took a slow sip of his seltzer.

"How have you been feeling lately?" She pouted sympathetically.

"Great." He winked at Massie.

She giggled, then casually unzipped her navy cashmere hoodie, revealing a tight white Stella McCartney tee with a metallic-gold horse decal across the center. Its boxy bottom barely touched her narrow hips, revealing a sliver of flat abs before the top of her gray knit leggings kicked in.

Claire exchanged glances with the Pretty Committee, silently asking if something was going on between Massie and Chris that she didn't know about. They shrugged, indicating they were just as baffled as she was.

"Feel like celebrating?" Skye tilted her head toward her shoulder and batted her green-mascara-covered lashes.

"Maybe," Chris answered with playful curiosity.

Obviously grateful for this live demonstration of Flirting for Dummies, the Pretty Committee stared, shamelessly shoving anyone aside who threatened their view.

"Well, I have just the thing." Skye inched toward him.

"Really?" Chris pulled the blue straw out of his seltzer and stuck it in his mouth.

Skye pulled the straw out from between his teeth and tapped it against her Angie lips. "Yup."

Chris blushed.

Massie stepped back to give them space. Or was she feeling left out? Claire had no idea, since, as always, the alpha's expression gave nothing away. Her amber eyes were fixed and steady—not angry or sad or happy. Just blank, quietly observing and absorbing. Was she jealous? Relieved that her plan was working? Or crushed that Skye had captivated Chris with so little effort. It was impossible to tell.

"I'm having an exclusive end-of-the-year party," Skye continued, steadying herself against the flow of party traffic.

"I know. I heard some of the guys talking about it."

"I bet you did." Skye stuck the straw back in his mouth.

Chris stared into her eyes.

Massie half-smiled. Her plan was working and she seemed relieved. If jealousy was an issue, she was hiding it like an unsightly panty line.

But before any deals were sealed, a teenage boy's voice crackled through the band's speakers and hijacked the moment.

"Ladies and gentlemen, can I have your attention, please?"

"It's starting," squealed the DSL Dater with the Swiss Miss braids. "Let's move closer to the surfers."

Skye leaned into the Pretty Committee's tight circle. "I'm going to leave. It's more alluring."

"But—" Massie tried.

"But nothing. Close the deal for me."

"But—"

"Tick . . . tick . . . tick . . ." was all Skye said before a pack of boy-crazy blondes tugged her toward the front of the crowd.

Derrington, Josh, and Cam hovered around the Pretty

Committee's closed circle like the rings of Saturn, probably envying Chris Abeley, Plovert, and Kemp, all of whom had somehow scored a place inside. Part of Claire wanted to grab Cam's leather-clad arm, drag him closer to her side, and inhale his Drakkar Noir. The other part wanted to chuck a bottle of sea-foam-flavored seltzer in his face. But all she could do was circle the anger cul-de-sac and continue avoiding him until she happened upon a way out.

"So are *you* going to her party?" Chris pushed up the sleeves of his brown henley.

"Given." Massie flicked the gold zipper on her navy cashmere cardigan.

"It's been a while since I've been in the mood for a party." Chris looked straight at her. "But thanks to you, I'm starting to feel ready again."

"Cool." Massie turned to the podium as if she didn't want to miss a single word of the dedication. She knew it would have been the perfect time to promote Skye, but her gloss was fading. And without its shiny protective shield, she felt vulnerable. Pretending to cough, she turned her head to the side and applied an emergency coat of Sugar Cookie Glossip Girl. *Now* she was ready to close.

"Well, I'm gonna go up front with my buddies. Let's talk later." Chris smile-winked, then forced his way through the audience.

Massie was about to reach out to stop him when Derrington crept up behind her and covered her eyes.

"Guess who?" he asked in a little girl's voice.

"Let go." Massie pulled his palms off her face. She unstuck her lashes, then searched for Chris. But he was gone.

"What's up with *her* highlights?" Derrington laughed so hard he snorted.

Cam and Josh cracked up and high-fived him.

Claire rolled her eyes. Was Cam always this immature?

"I'm moving up front," Massie announced. "Alicia, you're in charge. Make sure the mission is accomplished by the time I get back."

"Maybe you should stay," Claire heard herself say.

"Why?" Alicia adjusted the wide brocade collar on her short-sleeved ivory peacoat. "You don't think I can handle being in charge?"

Claire's heart quickened. "It's not that. It's just that . . ." She side-glanced at Cam, who was still whooping it up with the boys. He seemed like a total stranger—a typical boy instead of the loyal sweetheart she'd thought he was—and Claire had no idea how to approach him. Or if she even wanted to.

"She's right," Kristen chimed in. "We could use some support." She tilted her head toward Griffin, who was wearing black skinny jeans and a baggy white tee with a picture of a bloody headless Barbie doll on the front. He was leaning against a speaker in the far corner of the roof that was twice his height.

"What's wrong with *me*?" whined Alicia.

"Do *you* know what I should say to Griffin?"

Alicia looked to the back of the room and studied the aloof death-metal maniac. "Point." She gripped Massie's wrist. "Maybe you *should* stay."

"I can't." Massie wiggled free. "You don't understand. I have to find *Chris*." She mouthed his name so Derrington wouldn't hear, leading Claire to wonder if she had something to hide.

The bleached-blond beach stud at the podium tapped the microphone and demanded attention. His short-sleeved green-and-beige madras shirt was completely unbuttoned, exposing his well-defined chest, peanut-butter-colored tan, and rugged tangle of shark-tooth necklaces nestled between his collarbones.

"Good luck." Massie waved and then took off into the crowd.

"Hey. For those of you who don't know me, my name is Dune Baxter, and after five years of surfing the epic North Shore of Hawaii, I'll be spending the summer on this roof, as an instructor at the Briarwood Surf Camp, or B.S. Camp, as I like to call it."

The DSL Daters screamed in approval.

He snickered with fake modesty until they stopped.

"But this is not about me. It's about your new wave pool—" The crowd cut him off with applause. "Which your parents are probably paying tons of money for so you country-club punks can learn how to ride."

He ran a hand through his beachy, top-heavy hair while the crowd applauded again.

Cam gently shoulder-squeezed his way past Kristen and Alicia so he could stand beside Claire. A powerful magnetic force drew her closer to him (chemistry?), but she managed to resist its pull and stand firm.

"I kinda wish I was staying here this summer." He rested his elbow on her shoulder.

Claire turned and looked into his eyes for the first time all night. Had she been wrong about him and Nikki? Was this all just one big misunderstanding? Was Cam Fisher the same sweet guy she'd always thought he was? Hopefully. But she needed to be certain before letting down her guard.

"*Why* do you want to stay here?" She crossed her fingers for luck.

"So I can learn to surf," he answered, as if it should have been obvious.

"Seriously?" A combination of anger and pain welled up inside Claire. She clenched her fists, but the emotions managed to escape anyway.

"So, you'd give up camp for *surfing* but not *me*?"

Cam panic-blinked, and Claire instantly regretted her outburst. Would he write about it in his journal? Tell the guys in ESP? Laugh about it with Nikki? She shook the thoughts from her head, but they wouldn't leave.

"What are you *talking* about?" Cam removed his elbow from her shoulder and shoved his hands deep into the side pockets of his jeans.

Unsure of what to say next, Claire bit her bottom lip and focused on Dune. Cam did the same. It was the first time she'd ever played the role of the "needy girlfriend," and she could tell by his silence he was just as shocked by her response as she was.

"Here to start the flow of water that will fill Briarwood

Academy's brand-new epic rooftop wave pool is none other than five-time world surfing champ Brice Baxter."

Flashbulbs flashed and the crowd cheered as Brice, a larger, tanner, toner version of his son, appeared from behind the podium. He hiked up his loose gold board shorts and ambled over to the silver faucet at the head of the pool. Hand on the round dial, he lifted his head and smiled with pride for a round of pictures. Then he struggle-turned, an obvious excuse to flex his bulging muscles. Water vomited forth from the nozzle. The crowd cheered and the band of penguins struck up a jazzy version of "Singin' in the Rain."

"It's time," Alicia informed the girls.

Claire felt a stab of panic in her chest. How could she ask Cam to be her date *now*?

Luckily, Dylan made the first move. She lifted her arms like a phoenix rising from the ashes and wrapped them around Kemp and Plovert's shoulders. "Do you guys want to escort me to Skye Hamilton's costume party Saturday night?"

"Both of us?" Kemp adjusted his orange-and-gray Kangol, which had been accidentally knocked out of place by a passing mermaid.

"As dates?" Plovert removed his glasses and cleaned them with the bottom of his navy-and-yellow plaid button-down.

"Yeah."

"I'm in." Kemp grabbed Dylan's hand, then immediately let go.

"Me too." Plovert put his glasses back on.

"Done and done." Dylan winked at Alicia, then pushed

through the thick crowd and steered her boyfriends toward the sorbet table by the band.

"Did that just happen?" Josh asked Cam.

Cam shrugged, his green eye and his blue eye still fixed forward.

"Ehmagawd," Alicia interrupted. "Did you know we're, like, wearing the same white Polo again?"

"What do you mean, *again*?" asked Josh.

"Um . . ." Alicia blushed when she realized she had accidentally hinted at the secret Share Bear camera. "I mean, again and again I am amazed that we are wearing the same shirt."

"Mine is for boys." Josh was quick to defend himself.

"I love making people do chores for me," Alicia blurted, obviously desperate for a new angle.

Josh took off his New York Yankees cap. "Same here!" He peeked over his shoulder, then lowered his voice to a paranoid whisper. "Same here."

"Really?" Alicia squinted, like she couldn't believe the coincidence. "That's so weird."

"Ehmagawd," Kristen interrupted by slapping Josh's arm. "Do you know that guy?" She pointed at the giant speaker in the corner behind them.

He turned. "You mean Griffin?"

Kristen nodded, never taking her eyes off her black-haired, pale-skinned crush.

"Yeah, he's in my—" Josh caught himself. "He's in one of my classes."

"Can you introduce me?"

Josh shrugged.

"Hey, Griff, this is Kristen." He angled his thumb toward her cheek.

Without waiting for a response, Josh turned back to Alicia.

"Hey." Griffin waved, each one of his fingers adorned with a different skull ring.

"Do you read?" she shouted above the final chorus of "Singin' in the Rain."

Griffin nodded suspiciously.

"Because I am such a sucker for a sad story."

"What?" he called.

Claire couldn't take it anymore. ESP wasn't helping them. It was turning them into a bunch of idiots.

"I feel sick," she announced, clutching her stomach.

"Huh?" Cam finally turned to face her, but it was too little too late.

"I'll call you later." Claire bolted across the dance floor, weaving among rhythmless parents who were twirling each other across the makeshift wood floor as if scouts for *Dancing with the Stars* had dropped by for an impromptu audition.

"Wait!" he called.

But Claire kept on running.

How could he be so two-faced? Maybe Layne was right. Maybe Cam Fisher was a serial killer.

"Claire, stop!" He grabbed her arm. "Are you mad at me? Because I didn't mean I'd rather surf than spend the summer with you. I was just saying—"

Unable to speak without sobbing, Claire shook her head no, trying to tell Cam he had it all wrong.

"Headache." She covered her face with an icy palm.

"Maybe this will help," Cam reached into the pocket of his leather jacket. He opened his palm, revealing a brown leather bracelet with three black-and-white letter blocks in the center. They spelled I ♥ U.

Claire stared at it, no longer able to hold back her tears.

"I'm glad you like it." He beamed, mistaking her watering eyes for joy.

Pinching the leather strap from his palm, Claire studied it *CSI*-style. Had Nikki touched the worn leather in the same spot she was touching it now? Did it smell like her perfume? Had she made it at camp or bough it at the mall?

"Wanna know how much I like it?" Claire heard her voice shake, the bracelet trembling in her hands.

Cam inched closer, preparing for a thank-you peck.

"This much!" She whipped it into the wave pool and stormed off toward any place that was not right there.

"Why'd ya do that?" Cam called, his voice cracking. "What's wrong?"

But Claire kept running toward the Pretty Committee, who were still on the far side of the dance floor, flirting with their potential HARTs.

"I don't understand you!" he shouted again. This time, the boys heard. Derrington said something to Josh, who said something to Griffin. They quickly waved good-bye to the girls and hurried toward Cam, who was heading for the stairwell.

"Nice going, Claire." Alicia rested a hand on her shoulder.

Claire felt a wash of relief. At least she had the support of her friends.

"Where did the boys go?" Massie asked Alicia as she squeezed her way back into their tight circle after her latest attempt to force Chris and Skye together. "Mission accomplished or what? Does everyone have a date?"

Alicia lowered her eyes. "It wasn't my fault," she whined. "Josh ran over to Cam before I could ask him."

"Griffin too."

"Oh." Claire blinked back the tears that had transformed the well-dressed party guests into blurry blobs. "So that's what you meant by 'nice going.'"

"Um, yeah. Did you actually think I was serious?"

"Did Chris ask Skye?" Kristen asked eagerly.

Massie tugged on her charm bracelet and shook her head. "I couldn't find him for the longest time and then . . ." She paused, as if the rest were too painful to discuss.

"What? What happened?" asked Alicia, sounding relieved she wasn't the only one who'd failed.

Massie angled her chin toward the band, where Chris was strumming a guitar, a yellow beak tied to his mouth and a cluster of love-struck blondes dancing at his feet. "So Dylan is the only one with a date?"

"Dates," Dylan burp-corrected.

The girls nodded shamefacedly as the band transitioned into "Bridge Over Troubled Water."

"Ehmagawd." Massie sighed. "We're. So. Done."

Claire thought of her leather love bracelet at the bottom of the wave pool and knew that once again Massie Block was right.

If ever there was a perfect moment to have 24/7 access to the bomb shelter, it would have been now. The Pretty Committee desperately needed privacy for what they were about to do, something OCD's crowded front lawn didn't provide during lunch period. But the Café had a strict no-phone policy, meaning table eighteen wasn't an option. So there they were, huddled under Massie's favorite oak, under a canopy of leaves, sitting on their hands to avoid grass stains and nervously picking at their low-fat turkey wraps.

Clusters of wannabes casually strolled by, side-glancing, hoping to overhear a mere syllable or two of alpha gossip. But Massie saw to it that her girls were seated knee-to-knee in a tight downwind-facing circle.

"Failure to secure a date for Skye's costume party before next period will result in a two-week suspension from my Friday-night sleepovers. Ah-greed?" Massie held out her pinky.

"Ah-greed." The girls locked fingers and shook.

"Here we go." Massie dumped the contents of her Dolce & Gabbana zebra-print tote on the grass. Out came:

- Four loose tubes of Glossip Girl (Cinnabon, Crème Brûlée, Candy Cane, and Original Bubble Gum)

- One pack of Dentyne Fire
- Estate keys on a red Coach picture-frame key ring—Bean's photo on one side and Brownie's on the other.
- A red-and-brown Coach Hamptons wallet stuffed with yellow Visa receipts.
- A Tiffany silver heart clip ballpoint pen
- A brushed-silver antique business-card holder loaded with the numbers of her favorite store managers
- A 0.25-oz. bottle of Chanel No. 5
- A YSL compact mirror (compliments of Gavin at the YSL counter at Barneys)
- A Red iPod Nano
- Bose noise-reduction earphones
- Oversize black-and-white Prada sunglasses (backup pair)
- A bottle of Evian water
- Evian mineral-water facial spray
- Purple Essie nail polish (#353, Munis Mauve, used mostly for highlighting important sentences in textbooks)
- An Essie Crystal nail file
- Clinique cuticle cream
- Six grape-scented pens (imported from London)
- The Jakkob Salon hairbrush (model #2865)
- Miss Groovy snag-free hair elastics
- Duane Reade bobby pins
- Bumble and Bumble Does It All styling spray
- A silver Motorola Razr
- A Palm Tungsten E2
- Six blue packets of Equal

- A Caramel Nut Brownie Luna Bar
- Skye's ah-nnoying watch

"Cell phones, please." Massie jiggled her empty tote in front of their faces.

Claire ripped a chunk of grass from the ground and released it into the breeze.

Dylan tossed in her mint-green LG Chocolate phone.

"You already *have* a date," Massie snapped.

"She has *two*," Kristen corrected.

"So true." Dylan stuck her tongue out at Alicia and then removed her phone with an exaggerated grab. "My bad."

"Kuh-laire. Kristen. Leesh. Phones! Now!" Massie unzipped her steel-blue Stella McCartney one-piece jumper, revealing the top of her white Splendid beater. Something was making her sweat. Maybe the midday sun. Maybe Skye. Probably both.

"Now?" Alicia removed her mauve cardigan (part of her new ultra-girly sweater set) and tied it around her shoulders. "We can't text them *now*."

"Why nawt?" Massie heard the panic in her voice. "The party is in two days. It's time!"

"But it's so bright out here." Alicia made a show of squinting and then lowered the brim on Josh's New York Yankees hat. "The glare will make it hard to read the screens, and we may type the wrong thing by accident."

"What are you so afraid of? You're wearing his hat. He ah-bviously likes you." Kristen took a long swig of Gatorade

Fierce, accidentally dribbling blue on her copy of *The Note-book.* "Shoot!"

"I know he *likes* me." Alicia rolled her big brown eyes in a "duh" sort of way. "But it's not ladylike for a girl to make the first move."

"Um, Martha *Ew*-art, what did you do with my friend Alicia?" Dylan bit into a Philly cheese steak sandwich. A glob of cheddar-soaked onions farted out the bottom of her hoagie and splattered onto her faded Lucky Brand denim skirt. She flicked it onto the grass with an L-shaped twig.

"Okay, Pig Newton, what did you do with my friend Dylan?"

Massie steamed like an Aveda facial.

"E-nuff!" she shouted. "Last phone in gets traded for a Nokia."

Seconds later, her Dolce & Gabbana zebra-print tote contained five cell phones.

"Here I go." She closed her eyes and reached inside.

"No fair," Alicia blurted. "You know the feel of your own phone. You're gonna pick yourself last."

"Alicia, are you a soccer coach for chickens?"

"No." Alicia lowered the brim of Josh's black NYY hat.

"Then why are you calling fowl play?"

Kristen and Dylan burst out laughing.

Massie dug her hand into the bag again.

"I'm just saying, you *could* fix it so that you can feel—"

"Um, my eyes are closed, remember?" Massie snapped, hoping Alicia was too rattled to realize that that didn't make any sense. "Here I go." She turned her head away from the bag, reached inside, and pulled out a thin silver cell.

"Alicia!" She grimaced and handed her the secret underground Briarwood Academy directory, a complete list of all the boys' e-mail addresses, cell numbers, and screen names, compiled by a mysterious source and downloadable for just thirty dollars on J-adoreBboys.com.

"Fine." Alicia grabbed her phone, then the directory. Her thumbs scuttled across her flat keypad. When she was done, she read her message aloud. "Alicia Rivera is requesting ur company @ a famous couples costume fete sat. nite. U can B Ralph Lauren and I'll B his wife, Ricky. RSVP ASAP."

Massie made a fist and stamped the ground. "Ah-pproved."

"Send." Alicia dug her French-manicured thumbnail into the keypad, snapped her cell shut, and rested it on her white-linen-clad thigh.

Next, Massie pulled out Kristen's black Razr (a recent hand-me-down from Massie). After a quick scan of the Briarwood directory, Kristen started dialing. She covered the mouthpiece once she noticed her friends looking at her in curiosity. "He's a romantic. Talking is more intimate than texts. Trust me." The side of her jaw twitched as she waited for him to answer.

The Pretty Committee leaned forward in anticipation.

Kristen suddenly finger-combed her blond hair. "Um, hey, Griffin, it's Kristen." She paused. "Gregory. You know, from the wave-pool dedication ceremony last night?" She nodded yes. "Right, the one with the reading obsession." She flashed the girls a triumphant thumbs-up. "Well, I was invited to an eighth-grade costume party Saturday night, and the theme is famous couples. And I thought maybe you'd want to go with me. You can be Noah and I'll be Allie—you know, from *The Notebook*? The novel, not the movie, of course."

Kristen's aqua-blue eyes darted from side to side while she listened. "Um, no, the costumes aren't supposed to be boring. Why?"

The girls covered their mouths and giggled. Kristen kicked them. Dylan grabbed her leg and pulled off one of her orange-and-turquoise Pumas and whipped it across the lawn. Everyone burst into muffled hysterics, even mopey Claire.

"Oh. I see." Kristen covered her left ear, trying her hardest to stay focused. "Yeah, that sounds great. I would love to go as the Bride of Chucky. And you'll be . . ." She paused. "Sure, of course. You'll be Chucky. Makes perfect sense. Okay, well, I'll call you Saturday with the details. . . . Oh, texting is fine? Great. Works for me. Okay, 'bye." She snapped her phone shut and buried her blushing face in her black Prada messenger bag. "No one say a word," she moaned.

Everyone cracked up.

"Moving awn," Massie announced, once the laughter died. She pulled out Dylan's green cell and tossed it at her. "Stop wasting my time—you're already done."

Claire bit her thumbnail, knowing she was next.

"Here you go." Massie handed her the red Swarovski crystal-covered *Dial L for Loser* phone she'd gotten as a gift from Rupert Mann, the film's director.

Kristen sat back up and joined their tight circle, obviously thrilled that it was someone else's turn to make a fool of herself and that her moment had passed.

"I can't."

"You *have* to."

"I tossed the love bracelet Cam gave me in the wave pool last night, and we haven't talked since. How am I supposed to explain *that*?"

"Bad sushi," everyone said at once.

Claire giggle-sighed.

"It's not like he *bought* the bracelet. It was re-gifted," Alicia offered, trying to be helpful. "So you shouldn't feel bad about it."

"Um, thanks for reminding me." Claire pushed her paper plate aside. Her turkey wrap rolled onto the grass, but she ignored it.

"Ehmagawd!" Alicia waved her phone. "It's vibrating! What if it's Josh?" She fanned her cheeks like a Southern belle.

"What does it say?" Dylan reached for the phone, but Alicia pulled it away.

"It says *yes*." Alicia tightened her mouth into an *O*, obviously trying to hide her budding smile.

Everyone applauded and cheered.

Alicia turned to Claire with newfound confidence. "Come awn, text Cam. It's easy."

Claire chewed her bottom lip. "Fine."

They waited patiently while she typed.

Suddenly, the inside of Massie's D&G bag dinged. "Ehmagawd, it's a text from Chris Abeley."

"Read it!" everyone urged, slapping their thighs excitedly.

Massie's mouth suddenly went dry. She licked her lips, tasting the minty remnants of Candy Cane Glossip Girl.

"Uh-oh . . ." She read the message. "He wants me to go to the horse show with him Saturday night at Madison Square Garden."

The girls squealed with delight.

"*No*, you don't *get* it." Massie wiped her forehead with the back of her hand. "He needs to be at Skye's party Saturday night."

"Point." Alicia lifted her finger.

Massie exhaled and typed back.

"What are you gonna say?" Kristen leaned toward Massie's tiny screen.

"I'm inviting him to be my date for the party," she replied matter-of-factly.

A sudden gust of wind rattled the leaves above their heads, delivering a sudden chill to the air.

"What about Skye?" Alicia untied the mauve cardigan around her neck and slid it back on.

"And Derrington?" Dylan burped.

"And the bomb shelter?" Kristen added.

Claire bit her thumbnail.

"*Puh*-lease. I have a plan."

"What is it?" Alicia asked.

"Yup." Massie giggled.

No one laughed.

"Relax, I'll figure it out."

She texted Chris. SKYE'S PARTY. INTERESTED? was all she sent. He responded back immediately.

"He said *yes*." She waved her phone, temporarily forgetting that this was hardly a victory. After all, Chris should have been going with Skye. Not her.

Another text followed immediately. Massie read it aloud.

"'How 'bout I go as Romeo and U B Juliet. Not the Shakespeare ones, the Baz Luhrmann ones with Claire Danes and Leo DiCaprio. U wear angel wings and I'll wear a bloody shirt like Leo when he screamed, "I am fortune's fooooool."'"

SOUNDS GR8, she texted back with an eye roll.

"Chris should be the new model for Calvin Klein's Obsession." Alicia giggled.

Everyone high-fived her but Massie, who knew this situation was messed up and far from funny. Normally Chris's infatuation with her would be flattering times twenty, but in this case, it was a supermodel-size obstacle that was standing in the way of her alpha dreams. And despite Chris's ah-dorable haircut and ah-mazing blue eyes, she was starting to resent him.

"Now, Kuh-laire . . ." Massie checked the time on her cell phone. Six more minutes until the bell rang. "Are you going to text Cam or what?"

Claire looked up as if waking from a deep sleep. "I did. It

says, Sorry I took off. I 8 bad sushi and didn't want you 2 C me hurl—"

They giggled.

"Be my D8 at costume party Saturday nite and I'll make it up 2 U. U can B Adam and I'll B Eve, the 1st couple on earth."

A round of applause followed, bringing a much-needed smile to Claire's face.

Massie nodded with approval. "Send."

Claire did what she was told, then fell back onto the grass, hid her face in the crook of her elbow, and mumbled to herself.

Massie's cell dinged again.

"Chris *again*?" Alicia's brown eyes were wide with disbelief and envy.

"Ehmagawd, no!" Massie shouted at her screen. "It's Derrington."

Everyone leaned in.

Massie's head started to throb. She slid on her purple-lensed Chloé sunglasses, despite the shade, and read the text aloud. "'R u inviting me to that costume party or what? Everyone else is going.'"

"Ehmagawd." Dylan speed-clapped. "We'll both have two dates. Two dates will be the new one date."

"I *can't* have two dates." Massie rubbed her temples. "Chris needs to end up with Skye."

Claire lifted her phone above her head and muttered, "Cam said yes."

"What'd he write?" Alicia asked.

"'Forgiven. I'll bring the fig leaves.'"

"Cute!" Dylan put an arm around Claire and affectionately pulled her close. "Whatever." Claire rolled onto her side, her abandoned turkey wrap staring her straight in the eye.

"We better get to class." Kristen stood and brushed the grass off her navy Puma sweats. "We have two minutes."

"Wait! What am I going to tell Derrington?" Massie grabbed her ankle.

"Tell him you were just about to ask him," Kristen urged.

Massie exhaled sharply through her nose. Nothing said "rock bottom" like an alpha begging for boy advice. But then again, Skye had begged *her* for help at Galwaugh Farms.

The realization forced Massie to reevaluate: *Is emotional honesty in and fake confidence out?* Before she had a chance to fully contemplate this, she spotted Claire dabbing her bleeding cuticles with a leaf. And suddenly the answer was clear. Fake confidence was far more attractive.

And with that, Massie put the whole "issue thing" with Derrington aside (for now!) and texted him, asking if he would like to be David Beckham to her Victoria.

"Great costume idea." Kristen oozed jealousy.

"Seriously." Alicia stood, leaving her uneaten lunch behind for the birds. "Derrington thinks so." Massie wagged her phone facetiously.

With a tired sigh, Claire forced herself onto all fours and gathered the trash.

"One question." Dylan held out her hands and let Kristen pull her up.

"How are you going to fit angel wings under a tight Victoria Beckham shirt?"

"Puh-lease." Massie scooped up her loose belongings and dumped them into her tote. "That's the least of my problems."

"Hurry!" Claire squirmed while Massie worked the key in the lock of the bomb-shelter door.

Her urgency no longer stemmed from a fear of Principal Burns, Mr. Myner, or compost duty. Claire needed instant access to the room for one reason only—and that was to see how her story would end.

She'd felt the same way after the season-three finale of *The O.C.*, when Marissa Cooper died. She needed to know how the characters would process the tragedy. Needed to see how their stories would unfold, now that everything had changed. Needed to know if there was still a chance for a happy ending.

"We're in!" Massie pushed through the heavy door.

The salty, fishy smell of seaweed hit them like a tsunami when they entered. Brown-stained chopsticks, silver foil trays filled with drying wasabi, and red-and-white packets of Kikkoman soy sauce were scattered across the black rubber floor.

"Was Dylan already here?" Massie asked playfully, while clicking on the large-screen TV.

Claire tried to giggle, but she'd been frowning for the last forty-eight hours and her facial muscles seemed locked in a perma-pout. She was hoping a good episode of ESP—

one where Cam explained that Nikki was an eight-year-old camper he mentored—might loosen them back up.

"Have you noticed her face swelling?" Massie tightened the gold belt on her navy minidress and pulled up her faded jeans. "One more Philly cheese steak and she'll need to go up a size in sunglasses. Should we be worried?"

"About what?" Claire asked as she settled into the pink faux-fur chair, waiting for the picture to appear on the screen.

"Dylan!" Massie snapped. "She's been gaining weight. Haven't you noticed?"

Claire shrugged. Maybe Dylan's angular face was looking a little doughy lately, but so what? She was having fun. If doughy meant happy, Claire would take it any day over her current diet of tears and fingernails.

"Well, have you noticed Alicia's been acting like a grand-mother? And what about Kristen? One day it's death metal and the next it's—"

"Yes!" Claire interrupted, as the classroom flickered on-screen.

The picture flashed, scrambled, and faded. It made Claire think of a sneeze-tease, where you gasp and gasp and gasp and then, right when the tissue is in position, the sneeze disappears.

"What happened?" She jumped out of her director's chair and gripped the corners of the screen.

Massie aimed the rhinestone-covered remote at the lifeless monitor and clicked; it hummed like a rebooting computer.

"Give it a minute," she said to Claire's light blue Old Navy overalls. "Have you been wearing those all day?"

Claire looked down and nodded. "What's wrong with them? Dylan wore overalls last week and you said they were cute."

"Yeah, but hers were expensive." Massie shifted her bangs right with a delicate finger-swipe. "Don't you think it's kind of lame that they decided to stay in class? It's like they have their dates, so why bother? If I were them, I'd wanna find out what Derrington's issue is, or who Nikki is, because I'm a good friend. But they ah-bviously care more about topsoil and manure than us. Which is fine. I'm just not going to tell them anything we hear."

Claire heard what Massie was saying in the same way she heard her parents' conversations through their thin bedroom wall: Her voice seemed distant, the words intended for someone other than her.

A vibrating cell phone put a sudden end to her chatter. Massie flipped open her Motorola and sighed.

Claire sneaked a peek at the message, which simply said, "Tick . . . tick . . . tick."

"What are you going to do about Chris and Skye?" Claire asked, in an effort to care about something other than Cam.

"This." Massie pulled a crumpled note out of her AG jeans pocket and handed it over.

Claire unfolded the lined paper and read. The handwriting looked like Massie's, only thinner, and the letters were smashed together, boy-style.

Angie,

I'll be at your party. I'll be the guy dressed in a white shirt with blood all over it, because my heart bleeds for you. Can't wait!

xoxo Brad (Chris Abeley)

PS—Once again, don't mention this note. I'm still very, very shy.

Claire handed it back.

Massie jammed it back in her pocket. "I'll give it to her after class," she explained, as if she were reading Claire's mind. "It's the only way."

"Sounds good," Claire said . . . or maybe she just thought it. It was hard to know for sure, because the picture came back on the monitor, and everything else fell away.

A shaggy black hair-wall hung over Griffin's face as he read under his desk. Plovert and Kemp were seated peacefully beside each other; Josh was hatless, since Alicia was now a fan of New York Yankees caps; and Derrington was painting his nails with Wite-Out. The only person Claire couldn't see was Cam. Which meant . . .

"He's holding the bear!"

Claire couldn't believe her luck and timing. She was finally going to get the answers she needed.

"That was a great trust exercise," Dr. Loni's voice boomed, still from beyond the camera's reach. "Now that we're all warmed up, let's touch on some unresolved issues. I want to start with Derek's issue with May-ssie, and we will get to that next—"

"It's *Maa*-ssie!" she shouted at the screen. "And stop calling it an *issue!*"

"But first, it seems as though there was an incident between Cam and Claire the other night." Throats were cleared. Chairs creaked. "And I am very pleased that you boys pulled together and created a safe house for Cam and his feelings, which I understand were hurt very badly. Tell me, is it Nikki again?"

Claire's stomach lurched when she heard that name.

"It's awn." Massie leaned forward, like she was watching a suspenseful chase scene in a movie.

And then, in a single flash, everything went dark.

"What just happened?" Claire screeched.

Massie pressed her thumb into the remote with cuticle-whitening determination.

Nothing.

She pressed harder.

Nothing.

She gripped her charm bracelet, pinched the gold crown, and jammed one of the spires into the POWER button.

Nothing.

"It's dead," she announced. "Time of death: 2:27 p.m."

"It can't be."

"It is."

"Why is all of this *happening*?" Claire smashed her fist on the wood handrest of the director's chair. The throbbing ache that followed felt good, the same way getting punished for doing something terrible can sometimes be better than living silently with the guilt.

"Relax," Massie insisted. "All we have to do is get into that classroom and fix whatever broke."

"But the party's tomorrow night," Claire whimpered. "And now we're going to have to face Derrington and Cam without knowing—"

"You don't think I know *that*? You don't think I've spent the last three nights spritzing my pillowcase with Crabtree & Evelyn lavender sheet spray to help me relax? Derrington has an issue with me and everyone knows about it *but* me." Massie tried the remote one more time. But it was pointless. "Ugh!" She whipped it onto the floor and looked away in anger when the black plastic battery cover bounced off. After a deep, composing breath, she turned to Claire, her tone noticeably calmer. "We'll have to *file* until this camera is fixed."

"What?"

"File. Fake-smile."

"How are we going to do that?"

"What? File or fix the camera?"

"Both."

Massie tapped her fingernails against her pearly white teeth until her lips curled into a confident half-smile and her eyes lit up.

"Well, do you know?" Claire asked again.

"No." Massie marched to the exit. "But I bet Layne does."

"Layne?"

All of a sudden, Massie flicked off the lights, leaving Claire in the dark to wonder if she was, in any way possible, serious.

The Blocks' silver Range Rover glided over Briarwood Academy's dark, rain-slicked pavement.

"Isaac, kill the lights," Massie whisper-shouted from the backseat.

The driver did as he was told.

"Stop here."

Isaac shut off the engine near the statue of the Army Guy—a proud general (or officer or whatever) who saluted his invisible troops from an iron pedestal a few yards away from the front steps. Everyone in the backseat exchanged nervous glances.

"Is there a reason you girls need to accompany Todd inside?" Isaac put an arm around the back of the empty passenger seat, then craned his neck to face them. His graying brows were arched, his smile suspicious.

"I told you," Massie said wearily, "he forgot his science homework."

Isaac squinted, the crow's feet around his gray-blue eyes deepening. "Yes, but why are you *all* going?" He scanned everyone's outfits, as if questioning those more than their solidarity.

Massie peeked at the Pretty Committee. They *did* look

suspect in their black-on-black ensembles, smoky eye shadow, and nude lips.

Initially, the plan had been to tell Isaac they had been trying on outfits for an upcoming fashion-forward high school party. Then Layne had shown up wearing a plastic yellow miner's hat (complete with blinding headlight) and a thick tan leather tool belt. Fashion-forward in West Virginia, maybe. But Westchester? Definitely nawt!

And then there was Todd. A silver canteen was slung across his tan camouflage jumpsuit. Massie had made it perfectly clear that his role in the operation did not require undercover fatigues, yet he'd insisted. And seeing as he was a key player in their scheme, she'd been forced to let it go.

"Well?" Isaac pressed.

"Ehmagawd." Massie slapped a black satin Hermès-gloved hand against her heart. "Do you aw-nestly think his mother would want him going in there alone?" She gasped, as if they were parked outside Dracula's castle.

"Point," Alicia chimed in.

Massie nudged Claire, whose nose had been pressed up against the window like that of an anxious dog. "Time to get out."

"Huh?" Claire managed, her breath steaming up the window.

"Open the door," Massie insisted through gritted teeth. "Hurry." She glanced at Isaac, desperate to get out before he fired off another round of probing questions.

"Oh, right." Claire's blue eyes widened. Encircled by the dark, racoonish rings of MAC's Carbon shadow, they seemed brighter than usual, like one of Layne's glow-in-the-dark bedside dolls.

"Let's move!" Massie whisper-commanded once the door was open.

The girls filed out in silence.

"Meet you in the back lot at eight-thirty." Massie slammed the door shut. She wanted to take cover behind the Army Guy and review the plan one more time, but Isaac was lingering, so they casually made their way toward the entrance along the wet sidewalk.

"Why doesn't he trust us?" Dylan dumped a handful of Milk Duds in her mouth.

"Because we're *miners*." Layne pointed to her helmet and burst out laughing.

Claire and Todd giggled. Alicia, Kristen, and Dylan looked at Massie.

On a normal night, she would have knocked the hat right off Layne's head and tossed it under the crushing wheels of the Range Rover. But this night was far from normal. Normal would have been a night of goss'n'gloss at Massie's weekly sleepover. It would not have involved Todd. Or Layne. Or sneaking into Briarwood. Or Isaac rolling protectively alongside them as if they were running some dehydrating school-charity marathon.

"Is everyone cool with the plan?" Massie asked as she smiled and waved goodbye to her driver as they strolled.

"When can we take that picture of you kissing me?" Todd smeared original-flavor ChapStick across his brick-red lips.

The minty-medicine smell reminded Massie of her grand-father's back cream.

"No pictures till we're done."

"You promised if I got you into the school, you'd let me take a—"

"Are we in the school yet?" Massie waved her black-clad arm through the dark, humid air.

Todd shook his head, dropped the ChapStick in his deep back pocket, folded his arms across his chest, and gazed into the moonless sky.

Massie sighed. "Is everyone cool with the plan?"

"Cool," they all answered back.

"Then let's move."

Dozens of evenly spaced lampposts cast ivory circles across the grounds like a giant pearl necklace. It was the first time Massie had seen Briarwood after dark for something other than a fund-raising gala, and the reality was shocking. It was kind of like seeing an A-list actress in *Us Weekly* without makeup. With the lights off, the old buildings looked drab, sleepy, and slightly crazy. The rooftop wave pool, which was now covered by a big white bubble, looked like an overgrown water blister in need of a good pop. Only a dim yellow glow to the right of the oak doors, which blurred against the mist, loomed from the headmaster's office.

Massie led them up the steps to the main building and tried the door. Even though it was locked, she turned to give the thumbs-up to Isaac, who finally stepped on the gas and drove to the back lot.

"Ready, Layne?"

"Ready." She unwrapped a Slim Jim and handed it to Todd.

"Ready, Todd?"

He unscrewed the metal top on his canteen, threw back his head, and took a long swig. "Ahhhhhhh. Ready." He wiped his wet lips with the back of his hand and then winked. "This is for you, sweet cheeks. In case I don't make it back."

Todd lifted the canteen over his head and lowered it over Massie's shoulders.

"Ew." She batted it away. "Get it offa me."

She was about to rope it around his neck, but it was too late. Todd had turned to the tall wood doors and started banging.

"Stage one of the plan has been activated," Massie announced.

"Let me in! Please let me in."

The girls raced down the steps and hid in the shrubs, where the rain had kicked up the earthy smell of soil and leaves. Surrounded by darkness and heavy breathing, Massie fought the urge to imagine that she was being buried alive.

"Let me in! Please let me in," continued Todd. After a solid minute of bang-shouting, the doors clicked open.

The wrinkled night janitor popped his head out the door, smoothed a flap of greasy gray hair to the left side of his head, then cleared his throat. "Whatcha want?"

"I forgot my science book, and I have a big test on Monday. Can I just—"

"School's closed."

"But I need to get to my locker."

"Monday." The janitor shut the door.

Massie sent telepathic messages to Todd and marked them urgent.

Flatter him.

Threaten a lawsuit.

Kick him.

But Todd just stood there, chewing his bottom lip, as if looking pathetic and desperate might actually work.

"Ugh, why did I ever trust him?" Massie whipped his canteen into the bushes.

"He's doing exactly what you told him to do," Claire defended her little brother.

"I didn't tell him to buckle like a cheap sandal."

"Payless," Dylan burped.

"Shhhhhh," everyone whisper-giggled.

"Why was *her* burp funny and *my* miners joke wasn't?" Layne sounded genuinely confused.

"Shhhhh," they hissed.

"Wait!" Todd jammed his hiking boot in the doorway right before it closed. "I have a note."

"What?" Massie gasped from the bushes. "I never approved a note."

Todd reached into his side pocket and pulled out a lavender Marc Jacobs single-buckle coin purse.

Massie clutched the back pocket on her black Sass & Bides. "Ehmagawd!"

"Hey," Alicia whispered. "Isn't that your—"

"*Yes!*"

Todd unzipped the top and reached inside. "My note is from Mr. Franklin." He waved a crisp bill in front of the janitor's face like a victory flag. "And he has one hundred reasons why you should let me in."

The janitor snatched the bill from Todd's fingers and opened the door.

Massie air-clapped.

Dylan parted the bushes with both hands. "There he goes."

Todd jammed the Slim Jim between the two doors to keep them from locking once he stepped inside.

"Phase two, activated."

"Perfect." Massie air-clapped. "Come awn."

The girls crept up the steps and clustered behind Massie while she peered inside. The halls smelled like boy sweat and sneakers.

Hand-painted posters wishing fellow Briarwoodies a safe summer vacation made Massie's stomach dip. It was hard to believe the school year was almost over.

In the past, "over" had meant another job well done. Fun-filled memories. Hope for the future. But these days, "over" was starting to feel like plain old . . . over. As in Derrington thinking she was perfect was over. As in Skye and Chris were over. As in getting the key to the bomb shelter was over. As in dominating the eighth grade was over. As in Massie Block was over.

"Now where?"

"Sharp left up stairwell C. Top floor. East wing. Last room on the right." Kristen folded the napkin-map Todd had drawn for them with Massie's gray Nars eyeliner and jammed it into her black sock.

Massie gestured for them to follow her. After a single step, a bright light seared her eyeballs. She gasped. Who was it?

Isaac? The janitor? Campus security? Headmaster Adams? Dracula?

Either way, it meant the end of their mission and the start of her social demise.

"Why are we stopping?" whispered Layne. She searched the halls, taking the blinding beam with her.

"Ehmagawd, is that your hat?"

Layne turned to answer Massie, rendering her sightless once again.

"You should probably turn that off." Claire stepped in, obviously trying to prevent a smackdown.

There was a quick *click* and then darkness.

"Good. Now let's go!"

"Slow down," Alicia whisper-shouted. "You know I can't run."

"Shhhhhhh," the girls hissed back.

Everyone stopped in front of the windowless wood door at the very end of the hall. Panting, the girls huddled around the locked knob, wondering what to do next.

Massie signaled Layne with a sharp nod.

Layne nodded back and then reached into her tool belt and

pulled out a long necklace. It was made of different-size paper clips in an assortment of bright colors. "May I?" She pointed to her hat.

Massie checked over her shoulder and then nodded again. The light flicked on.

"Give her room." Massie pulled the girls away from the door.

First, Layne tried the small pink paper clip, then a medium white, a large green, a large silver, a small gold. . . . She finally found success with a jumbo metallic blue.

The door clicked open and the girls hurried inside. Layne clicked off her light.

Arranged in their usual semicircle configuration, the chairs faced a pea-green upholstered La-Z-Boy, which was occupied by the baby-blue Share Bear. Being there in person made Massie think of the first time she'd visited Dylan's mom at the *Daily Grind* studio. It had seemed smaller, less intimidating than it did on TV.

"It's nice to finally see this place in color," Alicia noted.

"You've seen this room before?" asked Layne.

"I mean," Alicia stammered, realizing her slip, "I mean, 'cause I got new color contacts, so now I can see color better."

"What?" Layne giggle-snorted.

"Hey, I thought I told you no questions," Massie hissed.

"Layne, come look at this library," Claire shouted from the back of the room. "Don't you collect self-help books?"

"No." Layne rolled her eyes. "Now, if I have this right, I am looking for a hidden camera, correct?"

"No, we *know* where the camera is." Massie sat in one of the chairs and crossed her legs.

"Where?"

"I said no questions," Massie snapped. "All you need to do is help us find the thing that makes the camera work."

"You mean the transmitter?"

"Whatevs." Massie slipped off her gloves.

"Well, those are usually hidden in walls." Layne flicked on her helmet light. "So everyone take a wall and start tapping. If it sounds hollow, move on." She pulled out a stethoscope, popped the ends in her ears, and pressed the chest piece against the eggshell-colored paint. "I'm only interested in areas of extreme density. Something that might suggest an inner panel of wires, cables, and/or high-speed—"

"Um, s'cuse me?" Massie cocked her brows. "Who made you alpha?"

Layne yanked the stethoscope from her ears, letting it dangle around her long neck. She turned to Massie, blinding her once again. "You did, when you gave me a video iPod and begged me to fix your mysterious don't-ask-me-any-questions camera. Now can we please get on with it? I'm playing e-chess with a Russian composer at ten."

Massie stood, silently vowing to stuff Layne in the compost bin as soon as this was over.

"Did you find anything yet?" Claire asked as she knocked on the back wall, which was covered in posters.

"Shhhh," Layne urged.

"Do you think this is going to work?"

"Shhhh!" Layne tapped her way across the empty wall to the left of the door.

"If this doesn't work, Cam and I are over," mumbled Claire.

"It better work." Massie fanned her cheeks with her gloves and crossed her other leg. "I need to know what lies Derrington's been spreading about me."

"Do you think we can still find a way to be eighth-grade boy experts without it?" asked Kristen, while tapping the chalkboard.

"Opposite of yes," muttered Alicia, who was walking along the windows, her hand cupped over her ear as though she were listening to a secret.

"Do you think Skye will blame the broken camera on *us*?" Kristen asked.

"Opposite of I hope so."

"Quiet, I hear something," Dylan whisper-shouted from the far corner of the room.

Layne hurried over and placed her stethoscope on the wall next to Dylan's hand.

"No, not *there*." Dylan pressed the chest piece against her stomach. "Here. Listen to that rumbling. I'm starving."

Layne pulled a Slim Jim out of her pocket and whipped it at Dylan.

"Just because *your* life isn't falling apart doesn't mean—"

"Relax, Kuh-laire." Dylan took a bite of the shriveled pepperoni stick. "Maybe if you loosened up and got in touch with your masculine side, this wouldn't be happening."

"This has nothing to do with—"

"Enough!" Layne snapped. "I've got something." She palmed the wall like a mime, higher and higher until she was balancing on her tippiest of tiptoes. "Someone bring me that chair!"

The Pretty Committee stared at her, refusing to take orders from an LBR, no matter how tech-savvy she might be.

"Hurry!" She upped her light to a brighter setting.

Claire dragged the chair to Layne and then handed her the blue Share Bear.

"Get this stupid thing outta my way." Layne whipped it across the room. Kristen intercepted it, head-butted it twice, then caught it World Cup–style. "If I can just get up to the ceiling, I think I can get to the main circuit breaker."

"The ceiling?" shrieked Kristen. "Since when are circuit breakers in the ceiling?"

"Um, why do you think they're called 'breakers'?" Layne asked.

The girls shrugged.

"Because people kept breaking them," she explained with a condescending eye roll. "That's why they moved them to the ceiling. To keep them safe." Layne stepped onto the arms of the chair for maximum height. Once steady, she pulled a mini pink drill from her tool belt, switched it on, and lifted the spinning spike above her head. "Can I get some spotters, please?"

Everyone gathered around the chair except Kristen, who was examining the Share Bear.

Layne began to drill.

Zzzzzzzzzzzzzz.

Massie grit her teeth against the sound, hoping to gawd it would not betray them.

Zzzzzzzzzzzz.

Zzzzzzzzzzzz.

Zzzzzzz-ping!

"What was that?" Massie gasped.

"I hit something metal." Layne wiped her forehead. "Probably an I-beam."

She drilled again.

Zzzzzzzzz.

Zzzzzzzzz.

Zzzzzzz-hisssss.

A light mist sprayed down on her hat, beaded off the plastic, and dripped onto the chair.

"Water pipe." She lowered her drill and rubbed her chin in confusion. "Let's move five paces left." She jumped to the ground.

"Maybe these are dead." Kristen held the Share Bear in one hand and two AA Duracell batteries in the other.

"Ehmagawd." Dylan covered her mouth for the first time all week.

The bottoms of Massie's feet tingled. Without a second thought, she grabbed Layne's helmet off her head and slid open the battery compartment. Two AA batteries rolled into her sweaty palms. She handed them to Kristen, who snapped them into place and slid the plastic cover back on the Share Bear's butt.

Claire chewed her thumbnail and toe-bounced with anticipation.

Kristen closed her eyes and flicked the switch. A green light popped on.

"Yes!" Massie and Claire hugged. Then they pulled in Kristen. Then Dylan.

Just then, the mist from the ceiling turned to drops.

"Told you I could help," Layne mumbled from outside the circle. "Don't worry about replacing the batteries. They're on me."

Then the drops turned to drizzle.

"What's *that*?" Dylan asked.

"Just some runoff from the pipes." Layne stuffed her drill back in her tool belt. "Unfortunately, it's typical in these prewar buildings."

Claire wanted to question Layne's runoff theory. But for the first time in a week something had gone her way, and she wasn't about to let a little thing like a leaky roof put a damper on things. As far as she could see, this problem was like wearing last year's jeans to a birthday party.

In a few days, all would be forgotten.

Wake up already!!!!! Come awn! How can you sleep when the hottest party of the year (not including the Oscars but yes, including the Golden Globes) is only 12 hours away?

Here is the prep schedule. Obey it or go bald.

	Kristen shoots video. (We must document this day)
9:30 a.m.	Meet at Block estate.
♥	Clothes: Mall sweats/tank (No black. I'm wearing black).
	Footwear: Knit Uggs, Havaianas flip-flops, Keds for you-know-who.
	Remember: Bring your own socks if you plan on buying shoes. Avoid borrowing the "sock of shame" at all costs. Those weird skin-colored tights carry foot lice. I read it in *Cosmo*.
9:45 a.m.	Stop at Sixbucks for ff lattes and scones.
10:00 a.m.	Isaac drops us at the mall.
	Claire shoots video.
10:03 a.m.	Shop for costumes.
	Alicia shoots video.
11:30 a.m.	Lunch @ Zodiac (mmmm, lump crab salad ☺).
	Dylan shoots video.
12:35 p.m.	More shopping.
1:50 p.m.	Ff lattes and biscotti for the car.
	Kristen shoots video.

2:00 p.m.	Isaac picks us up.
2:30 p.m.	Mani/pedis @ Avalon day spa.
	(No video. Too hard to shoot with wet nails.)
♥	Alicia, bring latest copies of *Us Weekly*, *OK!*, *Star*, and *Hello!* And all of the Hard Candy polish you swiped from the b _ _ b s _ _ _ _ _ r. (Busted! ☺)
	Alicia shoots video. (Get shots of finished nails and toes and of us entering the spa. No nudes, ew! Duh!)
4:00 p.m.	Spa/shower/shave at the Block estate.
4:40 p.m.	Give Isaac our sushi orders. (Keep it light to avoid bloating and massive Dylan-farts. ☺)
	Dylan shoots video.
4:45 p.m.	Jakkob @ the Block estate spa to do hair. Salma @ the Block estate to do makeup. (Robes and slippers compliments of the Blocks' spa. FYI, I burned a great prep mix, 75 minutes of nonstop party beats—awwww, yeah!)
5:00 p.m.	Text dates to confirm.
	Kristen shoots video.
5:45 p.m.	Light sushi dinner in the spa.
♥	Open wide, watch the makeup.
	Claire shoots video.
6:15 p.m.	Get dressed. (Jitters much???)
6:55 p.m.	My mom and dad want to take pictures (awwwww cute!).
7:00 p.m.	Isaac takes us to Skye's.
7:15 p.m.	Break HARTs' hearts!

Skye Hamilton's house had very little curb appeal. The yellow-and-white A-frame had a well-maintained garden and projected a cheery vibe, but no one was speed-dialing *Architectural Digest*. Typically, Sunday drivers tossed out words like *cozy* and *charming* when they passed. But tonight, traffic stopped.

The Pretty Committee, along with the other guests, entered on a red carpet that started at the foot of the short driveway, snaked through the narrow front hall, and led all the way to the recently renovated basement. The outside portion was roped off with gold stanchions, and Skye's parents, dressed as old-school journalists, snapped away as the eighth-grade celebrity couples entered.

Most of the girls had chosen costumes that required blond wigs, heavy eye makeup, tight tops, and micro-miniskirts, while the boys had opted for baggy jeans, gold chains, and slicked-back hair. Skye was one of the few girls in a dark wig, making her striking looks stand out even more.

Dressed as Angelina Jolie, she wore a tight black tank dress, to show off her henna tattoos, and black flip-flops. She carried four different colored dolls. Her big blue eyes appeared gray against the dark hair that framed her face, and her gawd-given puffy lips were perfect as they were. If her effortless beauty didn't make Chris fall for her, nothing would.

That was, if he decided to show up.

Guests made their way down the red-carpeted stairs and headed straight for the long snack table. They hovered around it, treating it like home base, while they dipped their chips and worked to steady their wobbling arms as they poured the punch. The lights were dim and the crowd was still thin, but the iPod DJ's purple laser-light show kept the energy level up—that and his club remix of Avril Lavigne's "Girlfriend."

Massie had been at the party for fifteen minutes and had managed to avoid Skye (so far) by pretending to be immersed in a life-or-death conversation with the Pretty Committee.

"Are you *sure* these Juliet angel wings don't look stupid over my top?" Massie grappled with the back of her tight white LaRok.

Like Victoria Beckham, she wore the crisp low-cut blouse with a black tie, a tipped fedora, gold satin short shorts, and knee-high Christian Louboutin platform boots.

"You look ah-mazing," Alicia assured her, for the nine hundredth time.

Massie had heard the same thing from Skye's parents, her friends, and some random girls at the party. Still, she tried to look utterly shocked to keep Skye from butting in. But there was only so long an old trick like that could fool an eighth-grade alpha. And the *clock* was ticking.

7:18 . . . 7:19 . . . 7:20 . . .

"Look who it is!" shrieked a DSL Dater dressed as a midriff-exposing Gwen Stefani (pre-baby). A rather plain guy with a slight wave to his hair, holding a small doll in a L.A.M.B. shopping bag linked his arm through hers—ah-bviously Gavin Rossdale and their son, Kingston.

"As usual, five girls and no guys. I wonder why?" She smacked her matte red lips together, then eyed Kristen, who was horrifying as the Bride of Chucky. "Hmmmm." She stared at Kristen's black motorcycle jacket, bloody scars, and pineapple-shaped matted blond wig.

"What?" Kristen snapped. "Not all of us use costume parties as an excuse to look like strippers."

"Well, you *should*."

"We *have* dates, you know," blurted Alicia who, as Ricky Lauren, wore a white cashmere beret and a matching floor-length sweater dress with a navy polo horse above her left boob. Even though Ralph's wife was blond, she'd decided to pass on the wig, because her shiny dark hair looked better with the outfit. And she was right. She looked like an RL model, not an RL wife.

"Actually . . ." Kristen zeroed in on the lone sand-colored beanbag stashed in the only corner of the room that wasn't occupied by clusters of shy party-phobes. "There's my Chucky now."

Griffin sat alone, reading. His thin torso curved like a parenthesis, and his face was even more scarred and bloodied than Kristen's.

"See ya!" She waved goodbye in a cocky eat-your-heart-out sort of way, which Massie hoped was intended for the DSL Dater and not her.

"You know"—Dylan put her arm around Massie—"some of us have *two* dates."

The DSL Dater searched the crowd. "You mean her and her?" A smile spread across her overly powdered face as she pointed to Alicia and Claire, then burst out laughing. Gavin Rossdale snickered, even though he probably had no clue what she was talking about. "Strut like you mean it, come on, come on," she sang as she pulled her date toward the dance floor.

"Where is *heeee*?" Massie wiggle-whined like she was holding in pee.

"Cam's not here either." Claire adjusted her leaf-covered bikini and repositioned the rubber python on her bare shoulder with a frustrated grunt, because it kept slipping onto her right boob. The Pretty Committee had persuaded her to dress as a sexy Eve so Cam would forget all about Nikki, at least for the night. And she'd decided she was desperate enough to go for it. "Not that it matters. I can't look at him without thinking of *her*."

"Ugh." Massie stomped her foot, totally ignoring Claire's comment. She glanced at the monitor, wondering if Chris had arrived, but all she saw were Dune Baxter and his surfing buddies walking the red carpet in nothing but board shorts and body oil. Skye and the DSL Daters greeted them with massive hug-squeals.

"He *needs* to be here." Massie peeked at the watch again, "Ehmagawd, two minutes."

"Don't take it personally. Guys are always late." Alicia sighed.

"Too true," added Dylan who was wearing a long black Demi Moore wig, big silver-framed sunglasses, and a white Armani pantsuit. "I'm still waiting for my Bruce Willis and Ashton Kutcher, and those two wouldn't blow me off if they were giving out free Nintendo Wii's next door." She sighed dreamily. "It's so great being the object of someone's obsession, isn't it? Especially when it's two someones." She nudged Massie's elbow as if she were the only other person on earth who could relate to such a rare dating phenomenon.

Massie made little effort to smile.

"Ehmagawd, here they are, coming down the steps." Dylan caught their attention with a frantic wave. Kemp was wearing a bald wig, and Plovert's dark hair was combed forward, grazing the top of his big aviators. "Hey, guys!" she burped, and raced over to greet them.

"Ew, what a turnoff!" Alicia winced just as Josh Hotz joined their tight circle.

"Hey." He nodded politely. A cloud of baby powder puffed off his head.

"Ehmagawd, you made your hair gray like Ralph's," Alicia gushed.

"And look." He pointed to his eyes. "Blue contacts."

"I heart that!" She scanned his costume: a navy blazer over a worn denim shirt, dark RL jeans, and cowboy boots. "Perfect."

"Hey, Ricky, wanna have our pictures taken?" he asked.

"Given." Alicia followed him upstairs.

"What if we *are* like the Cheetah Girls?" Claire asked Massie once the two of them were left behind, standing alone.

Her words cut like long Victoria Beckham nails.

Massie grabbed her cell phone and texted Chris a row of angry question marks. She hit SEND just as Cam and Derrington showed up.

The girls stiffened and *filed,* looking about as natural as Tara Reid's first boob job.

"Claire, can I talk to you for a minute?" Cam—whose Adam was more Tarzan, thanks to his tattered jean shorts and the clumps of grass shooting out from the pockets—clutched Claire's bronzed arm and pulled her toward the stairs.

"Can't you do it here?" She resisted. "They're gonna judge the costumes soon."

He ignored her pleas and kept tugging.

Claire looked back at Massie, her blue eyes begging for help. But Massie was checking her messages instead.

Zero.

She sent more question marks to Chris and then lifted her eyes. Only it was too late. Claire was gone. And Derrington had taken her place.

There they stood. Alone. No friends to hide behind, no first-crush giddiness to fuel them, no honesty. Just an invisible pile of secrets and lies that weighed so heavily on Massie's heart, it was hard for her to breathe. And the added pressure to keep her mouth shut and *file* made standing there with Derrington, face-to-face, amid the flashing laser lights and thumping music, more painful than a footful of new-shoe blisters.

"I got you something." He opened his fist and revealed two black-and-white soccer-ball earrings. They were amusement-park quality, and the posts weren't real silver. Still, Massie knew she should probably thank him anyway. But the earrings blurred into what looked like two melted bonbons as she stared and wondered why Chris was standing her up. Even though she needed him there for Skye, it was hard not to take his absence personally.

Derrington inched toward her and wiggled his butt like a happy bunny. "Cahn a wohld famous footballa get a thank-you kiss from his wife?" he asked in a terrible British accent.

"Thanks." Massie smacked his back like one of his soccer buddies would. If thoughts of the "issue" made making eye contact with Derrington unbearable, lip kissing was so not an option.

Derrington's puckered lips unpuckered, then wilted to a frown. "You've been kinda avoiding me all week. What's up?"

"Huh?" Massie checked the stairs for signs of Chris. If he was on his way down, she couldn't tell, because a dance train, led by a whooping Cleopatra, blocked her view.

"You haven't returned any of my texts, and tonight you're acting like you want to stop hanging out."

"Sorry. I didn't mean to make you think that," Massie told him.

And she didn't, exactly. Somewhere in the back of her mind, Massie had noticed how ah-dorable Derrington looked with his spiked blond hair, fake beard scruff, and silky navy-and-white Adidas Predator Beckham shorts with matching jersey. It was just that her mind was so occupied with the "issue," and Skye and Chris and the alarm on that stupid digital watch that she couldn't—

Rrrrrriiiiinnnnggggg.

Massie gasped. Prickly sweat stung her underarms. Her limbs froze with dread. And her lips begged for gloss.

"What's wrong?"

Derrington's voice sounded too distant to merit a response.

Massie searched for Skye. But all she noticed were people dancing, laughing, and enjoying their fabulous lives—three things she would probably never do again.

Rrrrrriiiiinnnnggggg.

Certain that by now Skye would be behind her, Massie checked over her shoulder.

But Skye wasn't there.

Chris was.

And he was holding his ringing cell phone.

"I just got your texts." He tried to smile but appeared too sad to pull it off. "Is everything okay?"

"Ehmagawd!" Massie threw her arms around him, paying no mind to the fake blood on his Romeo shirt and how that might stain her white LaRok. "I'm so glad you're here!" She pulled away and smiled.

"*'Ehmagawd, I'm so glad you're here'?*" Derrington squealed. "I'm not gonna stand here while you try to make me jealous." He jammed the soccer-ball earrings down the back of his pocketless shorts. One of them fell down his leg and landed on the floor. Derrington crushed it with his cleat. "I want a divorce!" He stomped off.

"Wait!" she shouted, and then made the snap decision to let him go. There would be plenty of time to patch things up with him later, if she even wanted to, but the clock was ticking on—

Bip, bip, bip, bip, bip, bip . . .

"What's that?" Chris rolled up the sleeves of his unbuttoned white Brooks Brothers oxford.

"Um, it's a special alarm." Massie fumbled around inside her clutch, feeling for the OFF button on the watch. "It beeps whenever a new clothing delivery has been made to Saks. It was a gift. From Saks, of course." She shrugged, as if owning such a gadget were no big deal.

"Cool," he said to the Roman sandals that crisscrossed up his mildly hairy calf.

"What's wrong?" Massie asked, momentarily forgetting what ESP had taught her about asking that question.

Chris tried to smile back but could only pull off a slight lip-twitch. His skin was pale, his fabulous Zac Efron hair was now flat, and his shoulders curved. The light behind his deep blue eyes was gone, like a dimmer switch had been turned too low. "Nothing. It's just weird being out again after . . ." He sighed, releasing whatever was bothering him in Skye's fruity-hair-spray-scented basement.

"Why don't you go say hi to the hostess?" suggested Massie.

"Not without my Juliet." Chris put his arm around her shoulder, accidentally jamming the wire from the wings into the back of her neck.

Massie wiggled free as fast as she could. Skye was bound to be looking for them now. And it would be best if they weren't touching when she found them.

"Hey, I made a cool playlist." Chris tapped the back pocket of his jeans, letting her know he'd brought it with him. "Maybe she'll let me plug it in."

"I'm *sure* she will," Massie trilled. "What's on it?" she asked, searching the crowd for Skye.

"Mostly ballads," he ho-hummed. "Perfect for slow dances."

"Sounds great." Massie turned away and rolled her eyes. Where *was* she? Where were her friends? Where was *anyone* who could save her from getting thrown from the top of the social ladder in the next ten seconds? The only familiar face she saw was Derrington's, and his toothy grin suggested he was getting on just fine without her.

He was by the DJ booth (a card table covered in a collage of glossy tabloid photos) surrounded by three eighth-grade pre-breakdown Britneys who were laughing their blond heads off, gripping their exposed stomachs, and swatting him playfully on the arm. One was even wearing the remaining soccerball earring, which slammed against her jaw like a wrecking ball every time he cracked her up.

Hmmmm. They didn't seem to think he was immature, and they were older. Massie couldn't help but wonder if she had been too quick to judge Derrington. After all, *CosmoGIRL!*

ranked sense of humor as the number-one quality girls wanted in their mates. And *CosmoGIRL!* never lied.

Finally, Skye made her way down the steps, one hand clutching the stem on her glass champagne flute and the other holding an armload of multiculti babies.

As if racing to catch a flight, Massie yanked Chris through the crowd toward the staircase, with no regard for who or what stood in their way. "Hey, Skye, look who's here," she panted.

"Oh, hey, welcome." She *filed,* then pushed past them.

"Wait!" Massie raced after Skye, leaving Chris by the stairs. This was hardly the reaction she expected from some-one who had been obsessing over—

And then it hit her. The realization made her scalp tingle-burn with fear and self-loathing.

Had Skye seen her hugging Chris? Had Derrington spread the word that Chris and Massie were Romeo and Juliet? Was she seconds away from over?

"Skye, wait! It's nawt like that." Massie followed her onto the dance floor like a desperate LBR. But she didn't care about appearances. Not at this precise moment, anyway. All she cared about was making things right with Skye, who clearly thought Massie was a boy-snatcher.

The first few beats of Justin Timblerlake's old song "Sexy-Back" throbbed through the speakers, and a loud, collective Six Flags roller-coaster scream followed. The DSL Daters rushed the dance floor, arms waving in the air and heads rocking from side to side. Within seconds Skye was enveloped in a circle of gyrating blondes. More than anything, Massie wanted to be surrounded by her BFFs, dancing freely, singing along, and giving the LBRs on the sidelines a fabulous show. But that would have to wait.

She forced her way into their circle and placed her hand on Skye's bobbing shoulder. "It's nawt what you think!"

"S'cuse me?" Skye opened her eyes but kept dancing. Pieces of her dark Angelina wig were stuck to her gloss, which she obviously didn't mind, because she made zero effort to remove them.

"I'm not into Chris. We're just friends. He likes *you*."

"Who?"

"CHRIS!"

"Um, okay." Skye twirled her body left and swung her head right. It was an advanced jazz move that Massie had only seen on Broadway.

"So you can have him." Massie gestured toward the lone guy leaning against the banister thumbing through his iPod.

"No thanks."

"Why?" It was Massie's turn to look confused. "I got him here before the alarm went off. He's in costume and he hasn't mentioned his ex-girlfriend all night. I think he's in a really good place."

"Seriously?" Skye finally pulled the black wig-hair off her lips. "That guy is such a downer. I like Dune now. Do you know him? Can you find out if he has a girlfriend in Hawaii or California or wherever he's from?" She spun again. "Not that I care. He's so delish I may have to go for him anyway."

A dancing Christina Aguilera accidentally elbowed Massie in the kidney. She elbowed back. Twice.

"Just like that? You're over him? After everything you made me—"

"What's the big deal?" Skye threw her arms in the air and clapped to the beat of the song.

Everyone joined in.

"Haven't you ever changed your mind about a guy before?" Skye squatted until she was practically sitting, then speed-thrusted her pelvis. "Oh, sorry, I forgot." Skye stood and spun. "I forgot. You're not ready for a serious relationship."

Massie stood over her, fighting the urge to introduce her next thrust to the heel of her Christian Louboutin platforms. "Do I still get the key to the room?"

"Of course." Skye spun. "A deal's a deal. Every alpha knows that."

"Great!" Massie beamed, and secretly tapped her thigh, congratulating herself on a job well done. The Pretty Committee had been granted full ESP access for the eighth grade. They could now add "boy experts" to their résumés, right after fashion consultants, socialites, tastemakers, and fabulous friends.

But the good news wasn't enough to keep Massie from wanting to punch Skye in her big fat Angelina lips. She resisted the urge, however, and stormed off the dance floor instead.

How could she have let the alpha use and abuse her like an LBR? Was it payback for all the times she had used and abused others? Impossible. Everyone she manipulated deserved it.

And there was nothing Massie had done to *deserve* what she had endured over the last two weeks. Nuh-thing. Skye needed to be medicated. It was as simple as that.

After a quick survey of the dance floor, to make sure no one was laughing at her, Massie straightened her bent angel wings, took three cleansing breaths, and made her way back to Chris, who was sitting on one of the bottom steps, squished to the side to let people pass. There was something about Skye not being into him anymore that made him seem slightly passé, like shrugs or peasant skirts.

"Did you ask her?" Chris looked up and ran his hand through his highlighted tips, which suddenly seemed awkward and inappropriate for Romeo—or any boy, for that matter.

"Ask her *what*?" Massie could hear the agitation in her voice, not that she cared. She needed more time to think, to process what had just happened. To heal.

"Did you ask her if she wanted to try my playlist?"

"Oh." Massie caught another glimpse of Derrington; he was surrounded by even more eighth-grade girls, wiggling his butt and making them giggle. She remembered how she used to laugh at his signature butt-shake and suddenly started to miss him. After all, he *was* a male alpha, a star goalie, ah-dorably adorable, and a www.awesomelip-kisser.com. If she *really* thought about it, how bad could his "issue" possibly be? Everyone *knew* Massie Block was as close to perfect as God would allow a human being to be. Sure, Chris had a driver's license and navy-blue eyes, but so what? Those qualities never even made *CosmoGIRLS!*'s Top Ten.

"Well, what did she say?"

"About what?"

"My *playlist*?"

"Oh, uh, she said maybe later."

"Great." Chris flashed a satisfied grin.

"Great." Massie rolled her eyes, knowing exactly why Juliet had killed herself.

CURRENT STATE OF THE UNION

IN	OUT
David & Victoria	Romeo & Juliet
Feeling stupid	Playing Cupid
Dune	Gloom

It was the perfect place for a make-out.

A vanilla Archipelago Botanicals candle flickered in its votive below the mirrored medicine cabinet, casting a warm fireplace-like glow throughout the cozy bathroom. Two hunter-green bath mats covered the tiled floor and felt like squishy moss beds under Claire's bare feet. And Cam agreed. It did feel like moss.

If it hadn't been for the toilet and the row of electric toothbrushes to the right of the sink, it would have been easy for Claire to imagine them standing in the Garden of Eden, the only two people on earth.

But in her current mind-set, Claire wanted to wrap Eve's rubber snake around Adam's Drakkar Noir–soaked neck and yank. Not even his ridiculous-in-a-cute-way costume could distract her from the pain she had been living with for the past week. But she would do her best to try. At least until she could get back in the bomb shelter and get the rest of the story. Until then, she vowed to act cool and carefree and—

"I know why you've been acting so weird lately." Cam stuck his index finger under the dripping faucet. He watched the drops gather, then spill into the porcelain sink.

Claire tried her hardest to breathe at a steady I'm-so-not-panicking pace. But her exposed stomach, which inflated and deflated faster than a blowfish with hiccups, betrayed her.

"You do?" Claire felt dizzy. She lowered herself to sit on the toilet seat but stopped halfway and stood back up. With all that was going on, the last thing she needed was for Cam to see how she looked going to the bathroom.

"I do."

Cam turned to her. His steady gaze, the gaze that usually made her insides warm, stopped her cold.

And then there was a knock on the door.

"Just a minute," Claire called politely, and then faced him again, trying to ignore her thumping heart. "Continue."

"Well, the summer's coming and . . ." He paused.

OMG! He was going to tell her about Nikki. How does one act shocked? Gasp? Widen eyes? Cover mouth? Clutch heart? Faint? What????

Claire tugged on an empty towel ring, as if it might open a trap door in the wall and give her a place to hide.

"The summer's coming and . . ." He paused again in the same place, like a scratched CD. Only this time he reached for her hand. "And you're pushing me away to protect yourself from the pain of being separated."

"Is that what your stupid, sensitive ESP class taught you? Because it's wrong! Not only is it wrong, but it's egotistical and conceited and . . . double wrong!" Claire wanted to scream. But she didn't. Instead, she stared into his green eye (she favored it slightly over his blue one) and willed her tears to go back to wherever they hung when they were off duty.

"So I got you something special." He leaned into the bath-tub and pulled out a tan Pottery Barn bag.

"How did that get in here?"

"Since the bracelet I got you is at the bottom of the wave pool"—Cam grinned, letting her know he wasn't holding any grudges—"here's something to remind you of me while I'm gone."

He handed her the gift.

She reached for it slowly, never taking her questioning eyes off his beaming face. *Another one from Nikki?*

Claire grabbed it and the rubber snake slid off her neck and plopped to the floor.

"Ahhhh!" The sudden thud made her scream. Then she giggled. Then Cam laughed.

His laugh reminded her of when they were happy. Then she remembered why she was sad. And she stopped giggling.

"Are you going to open the present or what?"

"What is it?" She pulled out a heavy rectangular object wrapped in red tissue paper.

"Is everything all right in there?" Skye's mother called from the other side of the door, her tone a mix of concern and suspicion.

"Yup," Claire called back cheerfully.

"It's that picture of us sharing that gummy worm like Lady and the Tramp, remember?" Cam beamed. "I blew it up and got it framed. I got one for myself, too. I'm going to take it to camp and put it right next to my—"

Claire stuffed the photo back in the bag without even

looking at it. The mere mention of the word *camp* made her—

There was a loud bang on the door. "Come on, I gotta *go*!"

"Well, *go* upstairs!" Claire kicked back.

"Buy some Pepto, loser." The guy made a fart sound, smacked the door, then stomped off.

"You're gonna have a picture of us at camp?" asked Claire, her insides quaking. An unstoppable emotional force, more powerful than her will to stay calm, was building deep within her.

Cam nodded slowly, suspecting he might have done something wrong—he just had no idea what.

"Won't Ni-*kki* mind?" Her face contorted like she'd just eaten a bag full of his re-gifted sours.

"Nikki?" Cam's eyes darkened. "How do you know about Nikki?"

Hearing him say her name out loud made Claire feel nauseated. Not a fleeting queasiness, more like a make-room-I'm-about-to-barf-the-California-roll-I-ate-before-the-party nauseated. She knew she was supposed to regret her outburst, but at the same time, it was a huge relief to come clean. And maybe now she could finally find out who the heck Nikki the camp tramp actually was.

Cam moved to the door and checked that it was locked, making it clear she wasn't going anywhere until he had answers.

"Did Derrington say something?"

Claire shook her head no.

"Then how?"

She still couldn't speak.

"You read my journal, didn't you?"

His voice was scarily calm.

"What?"

"You did. Admit it. At Slice of Heaven. When you took it into the bathroom. I was right. You read it."

Claire hated that he thought he was right to have suspected her. Because she hadn't really read his journal, at least not the way Cam thought she had. But she didn't bother correcting him. The more she thought about it, it was better to be a journal-reader than what she really was—a surveillance junkie, addicted to a spy camera in a blacked-out bomb shelter.

"Okay, fine, I read it in your journal." Claire looked down at her leaf green–painted toenails for effect. "Now can we please talk about it? Who is she? Do you love—"

"How could you do that to me? I trusted you." Cam tossed the beige Pottery Barn bag in the bathtub. The glass frame shattered.

The sudden noise and harsh gesture made Claire jump.

"Well, I trusted you, and you've been two-timing me."

Cam glared at her, searing her wide blue eyes with his anger. Claire felt a pinch in her throat. This whole thing seemed so unfair. She was the one who'd stood up to the girls in the bomb shelter and told them not to spy. And here she was, the only one paying for it. And the price was high. Higher than she ever could have imagined. This slight moral lapse was costing her true love.

"Is that what you think?"

She nodded, hot tears pouring down her cheeks.

"That's the trouble with snooping. You never get the whole story. And you know what? Now you never will." Cam pushed past her and unlocked the bathroom door.

"Wait!" Claire sob-begged as she reached for his arm.

But he was too fast. Ignoring her and the angry comments from the people waiting in line outside the door, Cam stormed off without another word.

Claire chased after him, wondering how they'd gone from being the perfect couple to *this?*

"Hey," someone shouted. "You forgot your snake!"

But Claire didn't care. All she wanted to do was find Cam and make everything okay again.

She finally caught up with him in Skye's spacious yellow-and-white country-style kitchen. The oval maple table was covered in leftover chicken wings and Hershey's Kisses, which Plovert and Kemp were helping themselves to.

An eighth-grade K-Fed, who was wearing a FedEx T-shirt, was describing Skye's bathroom to three of his buddies. They were whispering around a barrel filled with ice and cans of Red Bull but decided to leave when Cam barged in.

"I'm outta here," he announced, reaching for his leather jacket, which had been draped over one of the breakfast chairs.

"You seem bummed." Plovert popped an almond Kiss in his mouth. "I'll go with you."

"Me too," said Kemp, standing over the wings platter.

"S'cool guys," Cam tried smiling, to show Claire how good he could be at ignoring her. "Stay and have fun."

"But we don't *wanna* stay." Plovert looked over his shoulder. "Dylan is raiding the pantry as we speak, looking for ginger ale. She says the bubbles are great for burp contests."

"We can't take all the eating and burping and fart jokes anymore." Kemp waved the air. "It's like hanging out with Shrek."

"Cam," Claire said from the doorway, tired of feeling invisible, "can we just *talk?*"

He kept his back to her.

"Ugh!" Claire pretended to storm off by pounding her bare feet on the floor and then crouched behind the cooking island in the center of the kitchen and tried to steady her breathing.

"Can we get a ride?" Plovert whispered, his voice barely audible above the take-it-off chants and bouts of laughter wafting up from the basement.

Cam nodded.

"Me too?" Griffin crawled out from under the round breakfast table.

"How long have you been under there?" asked Kemp, pulling off his Bruce Willis bald wig and fluffing his shaggy curls.

"Twenty minutes," he whispered. "I'm hiding from Kristen. She keeps trying to make me talk about chick flicks like *The Notebook*. It's like she wants to bring out my sensitive side or something."

The boys burst out in hysterics.

"Did you tell her you don't have one?" Cam slapped his back.

"I told her I'm into the macabre and dark arts but for some reason, she's not buying it." Griffin pulled a fake Chucky scar off his cheek and flicked it onto a plate of brownies.

"She's almost as gullible as Dr. Loni." Plovert stuffed his Ashton Kutcher shades in his side pocket.

"Seriously, dude." Kemp snickered. "If he knew you fake-read romance novels to get an A in his class, he'd have an emotional breakdown."

"Well, let's hope he never finds out." Griffin opened the fridge, took a swig of Coke from the bottle, then jammed it back in. "It's the only class I'm not failing." He burped.

Claire's heart thumped along to the beat of "Glamorous," by Fergie, which was blasting downstairs. She wanted to grab Dylan and Kristen and tell them what she'd just heard before they humiliated themselves even more. But she was trapped, once again, with the burden of illegally obtained information, not to mention secretly crouched behind a cooking island.

All of a sudden, Massie appeared in the wood-paneled doorway, looking desperate and relieved at the same time, like she'd been running after a school bus and just made it. She noticed Claire immediately and gasp-giggled. Quickly, Claire lifted a finger to her lips, silently begging her not to give her away.

Massie zipped her lip and threw the invisible key over her

crumpled angel wings. Then, probably to avoid temptation, she helped herself to a seat at the table and re-glossed.

"Dude, eighth-grade chicks are awesome!" Derrington hurried in. "You guys have to come downstairs and hang. "They're totally easygoing. No head games. No random mood swings. No inside jokes. They're so much more ma—"

He stopped speaking when Kemp tilted his head toward Massie.

"So much more *what?*" Massie asked, pushing away the plate of wings like someone who had had enough. "So much more *what*?" She stood and placed her hands on her hips.

"Tell her, D." Kemp snickered.

"Yeah, tell her," echoed Plovert.

Derrington ran a hand through his bushy blond hair and blurted, "Mature, okay? They're so much more *mature*. There." He wiggled his butt. "I said it."

Claire silent-gasped, wishing she could see the expression on Massie's face.

"Um, excuse me." Massie cleared her throat, her voice steady and remarkably calm. "Are you a confused woman?"

"What? No, why?"

"Sorry, you look exactly like someone I know named Miss Taken." Massie tossed her hair.

The boys burst out laughing while Claire quickly covered her mouth and giggled into her clammy palm.

"*You* are the most immature guy I've ever met. You wiggle your butt to express your feelings, you wear shorts in the winter, you—"

"Whatever." Derrington swiveled his head to check out an eighth-grade Barbie doll who was returning a Bic pen and a pink sticky pad to the right of the cordless phone. Once she was gone, he turned back to Massie. "Go back to that *girl,* I mean *guy* with the highlights. I'm into older women now."

"Great." Massie tried to sound relieved. "I hope they like—"

"Are you okay?" Alicia burst into the kitchen. Josh was right behind her. "I saw you take off and run upstairs and I was worried something—"

"I'm fine times ten." Massie turned her back to the boys. "Never better."

"You coming?" Cam asked Josh.

"Depends," Josh said, releasing another Ralph Lauren baby powder puff into the tension-filled atmosphere. "Where's everyone going?"

"Away from these girls." Griffin shuddered. "I've never been more scared in my entire life."

Josh looked at Alicia with his blue contacts and smiled. "I think I'll stay and hang out for a while."

"Opposite of cool." Alicia stepped away from Josh and draped her arm over Massie's shoulder.

"Why?" Josh blanched.

"Puh-lease, I don't want to be the only one with a date."

"But—"

"Don't worry." She smiled a smile that was just for him. "I'll e-mail you as soon as I get home."

"'Kay." He snickered.

"'Kay." She giggled.

"Let's go." Cam led the angry boys out of the kitchen. "By the way," he called from the front door, "I see you behind that island, Claire. Are you ever gonna grow up and stop sneaking around?"

Claire's spine stiffened. Her cheeks flushed. She wanted to move back to Orlando. She had gone too far. There would be no turning him around now. And she hated herself more than she'd ever thought possible.

After the boys had left, Claire stood slowly and looked at Massie and Alicia in utter shame, regret, and embarrassment.

"Buuurrrrp!" Dylan emerged from the walk-in pantry holding a half-empty bottle of Canada Dry. She looked around the kitchen. "Where did everyone go?"

Kristen hurried into the kitchen carrying two champagne flutes. "Has anyone seen Griffin?"

"He's gone." Alicia squirted some MAC Lipglass on her finger, then spread it across her lips. "They're all gone."

Kristen and Dylan looked at each other in confusion.

"I told you not to act like a dude." Alicia rubbed her shiny lips together. "Your burp contest threw them over the edge."

"Wimps," Dylan burped.

"What about Griffin?" Kristen asked, placing the champagne flutes on the island. "Why did he leave?"

"His sensitive side was a scam to get a good grade in ESP," Claire explained.

"What?"

"The day he reads *The Notebook* is the day I read *Eragon*," Massie said.

"Gawd." Kristen ripped off her Chucky wig and tossed it into the plate-filled sink. "Never trust a guy in skinny jeans."

"Looks like it's just us girls again." Massie slid down the side of the natural-wood-colored island and slumped to the floor. Everyone joined her.

More bursts of laughter rose up from the basement, reminding the girls that the party was in full swing and that they were missing out.

After a moment of heavy silence, Massie cleared her throat and sang, "'Strut like you mean it, come on, come on.'"

The girls began to snicker. Then laugh. Then they doubled over in hysterics. They smacked one another's backs, gripped their aching stomachs, and wiped the giggle-tears off each other's cheeks.

Sure, they could have wasted the rest of the night analyzing their crushes and plotting ways to get them back. But come awn—that was so last week.

Claire leaned over the side of her bed and reached for her old Polaroid camera. Gripping it by the black strap, she hoisted it onto her tissue-covered lap. Then she sobbed a little more.

Once she was able to manipulate her pout back into a frown (slightly more flattering), she held the camera in front of her face and snapped. Seconds later a photo of herself, all puffy and snotty, rolled out. She labeled it post-party depression, then tossed it on the floor next to her leaf-covered bikini costume from the night before. Like Eve, she had given into temptation. And like Eve, she was doomed to pay the price.

A sharp triple knock on her bedroom door rose above the depressing R&B song on the radio about some girl who had done her man wrong and now it was too late for lovin'.

"Go away, Todd!" Claire yanked her blue star–covered duvet over her head.

"Relax," huffed Layne, letting herself in. "It's me."

Claire peeked out from her down-filled cave.

"I pedaled as fast as I could." She unfastened her sparkling green bike helmet, removed a pair of orange-tinted snowboarding goggles, and unrolled the rainbow-striped socks off the bottoms of her plaid pajama bottoms. "You're not gonna believe this." She unwrapped a Slim Jim, gripped it between her teeth, and hurried toward the Mac.

The sound of Layne's fingers scuttling across the keyboard reminded Claire of rain on the roof of a car. Which, for some random reason, made her cry all over again.

"Dry your tears, big ears, and come see this." Layne poked the enter key with gusto and folded her arms across her chest, the Slim Jim hanging from her lips like a cheap cigar.

"Just tell me," Claire moaned from her undercover cave. "I can't move."

Layne wheeled herself over to the clock radio that was still blaring the weepy song and hit OFF. "Not even to see Nikki's page on MySpace?"

"What?" Claire threw off her covers and shot up. A rush of dizziness forced her back down. Her head felt ten times heavier than usual despite all the stored water weight it had recently shed.

"Up, up, up," clapped Layne.

Claire stood, slowly this time, and realized she had to pee really badly. But that would have to wait. She shuffled stiffly toward her desk, hiding her fists in the sleeves of her lemon-yellow, gumdrop-covered flannel nightgown—the one she'd been wearing for the last fifteen hours.

"What are you talking about?" She leaned apprehensively over Layne's shoulder, catching a whiff of spicy beef.

"The other day I typed in 'Nikki.' Just 'Nikki.'" Layne blocked the screen with her oily, meat-scented palms. "But look what happens when I enter 'Nikki and Cam.'" She lifted her hands, revealing a picture of a girl with straight black hair and thick blunt bangs. She was either sultry/alluring or witchy/scary. It was hard to tell from the low-resolution photo. But one thing was very clear from her profile. This was the Nikki.

For starters, there was a Photoshopped image of a massive pine tree with two tiny heads nesting side by side in a nest on one of its branches. Written on the trunk in red cursive it said, *Nikki and Cam sitting in a tree*. To the left, typed over a navy background of twinkling stars and cricket noises, were all the answers she needed blogged out before her.

NAME: Nikki *wannabe* Fisher but *havetobe* Dalton.
AGE: 12
STATUS: Heartbroken
DATE: March 31st
TITLE: ***Final Entry***

I surrender.

I've rented every romance that Netflix has, like twice, and have tried every trick ever put on DVD. And nothing has worked. I even got a part in our school musical, hoping he'd quit soccer, transfer to Alvin Middle, and sing with me (luv u, Zac Efron!) But he didn't. I sent cinnamon hearts for Valentine's Day, gummy bears on Fridays, and a case of Jones Soda with a picture of us printed right on the label. (Remember the cute one I posted after the summer of us on the camp canoe docks, almost touching shoulders?)

Anyway, the flavor was 'crushed melon' since he

crushed me. But he didn't get it. The joke, I mean. He got the case, because I had the tracking number and tracked it, and someone named Harris Fisher signed for it, and I know that's his brother because I paid this online service to research his family tree. It was going to be his gift for Arbor Day. But I'm not doing that anymore. I'm not doing anything anymore. The crushed melon was the last thing I'll ever send him.

A week after Harris signed for the soda, Cam sent me an e-mail telling me "for the last time" to stop sending him things. He wants to be friends at camp, but he only wants one girlfriend and that's Cla---. (I can't type her name; it's too painful.) He told me he l--ed her (can't type the word; it hurts like mad). Then he said I have to respect that. And I have. Because love is all about respect. And I love him. So I have not sent another thing. Not even an IM.

Yes, of course I still check his horoscope (Taurus) and when I go under a bridge, I hold my breath and pray he'll have a crush on me this summer. But that's it.

Proud of me or what?

I will write again when I find a love who loves me back.

Broken + Heart = Nikki

Under her sad signature was a live counter that tallied the number of days she had gone without contacting Cam. And today, it said thirty-two.

"Well?" asked Layne, a gleaming smile carved across her cheeks.

"Thank you." Claire reached around Layne's back and squeezed. "You're the best!"

Layne, who was still facing the computer, gripped Claire's hands and squeezed back. "Cam's innocent!"

"Innocent!" Claire's teeth started to chatter.

Layne stood and spit out her Slim Jim, and the girls exchanged a real hug.

Colors and sensations returned to Claire's previously numb body, as though she had risen from the dead. She was starving.

"How happy are you?"

"So happy." Claire's teeth chattered harder. "I mean, he still re-gifted, but at least he's not cheating on—"

"No." Layne rolled her narrow green eyes. "You're missing the whole point."

Claire knit her light blond eyebrows.

"The bracelet. It's not from Nikki. It's from Cam!"

"You're right!" Claire air-clapped—then stopped when she realized that it no longer mattered. Cam was beyond mad at her. She knocked her head until it hurt. "I knew I shouldn't have spied. I knew it. I knew it. I knew it."

Layne checked her eyeball-hologram watch. "Gotta go." She jumped to her feet.

"Wait, you can't leave. You *have* to help me get Cam back."

"No can do, that's up to you." She giggled at her accidental rhyme. "My brother is going riding at two-thirty, and he wants me to dye his hair back to normal before he goes. A few of the guys were busting on his highlights at Skye's party, and now he doesn't want the stable hands to see them." She snapped on her helmet, pulled her socks up over her pj's, and lowered her goggles.

"'Kay." Claire managed an understanding smile. She thought about acting all sad and needy to guilt Layne into staying and helping. But her friend had done so much already. And she knew, despite the ache of loneliness in her body, that it would be unfair to hold her back. So, like Nikki, she swallowed her sorrow and said goodbye.

Once her door was shut, and after she peed, Claire dialed Cam. What she had to say was too important for texting, IM'ing, or e-mailing. It required intimacy. Of course, she couldn't confess to having watched his ESP class on a monitor, but she would apologize for reading his journal, chalk it up to a moment of insane insecurity, beg for his forgiveness, and promise never to doubt him or invade his privacy again. And she'd mean every word of it.

Hearing Cam's phone ring filled Claire with renewed hope. It had been weeks since she called him, and it felt good to imagine talking to him again. She was taking control. She would make things right. She had learned from her mistakes and was dying to share that with him. And when she was through explaining, he'd say he was still upset but was glad she called. He'd say he respected her honesty. He'd say he needed a little time to get over it. He'd say he'd call her after supper. And he would.

Claire was feeling better already.

Until she got his voice mail.

She hung up, waited ninety seconds, and then tried again.

And again.

And again.

And again.

After eleven straight attempts, Cam finally answered.

"Stop calling me!" was all he said.

Principal Burns stood at the podium shuffling papers while the OCD girls filed in. The auditorium smelled like wet textbooks, and the bands of colored light streaming through the stained-glass windows drew unfortunate attention to the major amounts of unsettled dust floating toward the dark, domed ceiling.

Once seated, everyone whisper-gossiped about what this impromptu assembly could possibly be about.

But not the Pretty Committee.

Dressed in head-to-toe gray—a sign of mourning—they had more pressing matters to discuss.

Kristen leaned forward, across Dylan, Alicia, and Massie, and gripped Claire's wrist. "Ehmagawd, I'm still in shock. He really said, 'Stop calling me!'?"

Claire averted her eyes and nodded yes. "Then he hung up."

"Well, that's better than getting your inbox flooded with flash-art pictures of pigs all weekend." Dylan sneaked a sip of Enviga, the calorie-burning soft drink.

"Well, I haven't heard a thing from Griffin, and I probably never will again." Kristen subconsciously rubbed her nail beds, which, despite three rounds of heavy-duty remover and a scrub brush, were still stained with black Bride of Chucky polish.

"What about Derrington?" Alicia asked Massie. "Has he texted you yet?"

"Um, not since I checked during the car ride over here," Massie snapped. "*He* thinks *I'm* immature, remember?" She rolled her eyes at the absurdity of it all.

"At least you have Chris Abeley to fall back on." Dylan sighed hopelessly. "I remember when I had two."

"I kinda got rid of him at the party." Massie lifted the cashmere fold of her gray turtleneck over her chin.

"What?" they all squealed.

"Why didn't you tell us?" Alicia seemed genuinely offended.

Massie shrugged, even though she knew why.

The truth was, she had forgotten all about Chris the minute Derrington told her off. And she had become obsessed with wanting to change his opinion of her. Obsessed with wanting him to like her more than the eighth-grade girls. And obsessed with figuring out the most "mature" way of getting him back. But why admit all that when it was cooler to act like it didn't mean enough to mention?

"It slipped my mind."

"How is that even possible?" Alicia's brown eyes widened. "He's cute and he drives."

"I know." Massie sighed. "But he's such a *downer*." She borrowed Skye's word, seeing as it was so appropriate.

"How'd you shake him?" Dylan asked. "He was so into you."

"I swiped his iPod, found the JoJo song that reminded him

of his ex, Fawn, and blasted it. Sent him right back into a full depression." She smiled with glee.

The girls leaned across one another for a group high-five.

"You know Colleen Campo?" asked Alicia.

The girls shook their heads no.

"Minnie Mouse?"

They nodded.

"I heard she doubled home on the back of Barbie's Ken's bike, and Mickey Mouse ended up crashing in Skye's downstairs bathroom because he was too embarrassed to leave without her."

"How upset was Barbie?" asked Kristen.

"Ew, puh-lease, *she* didn't care." Alicia rolled her eyes as if this should have been obvious. "Ken is her twin brother."

"I heard Emily Merlino told Rachel Brown that we had the cutest dates there," Alicia beamed.

"Until they bailed on us," Dylan whispered as she silently read the nutritional information on the back of her sparkling green tea drink.

"Shhhhh," Massie hissed, eye-warning her friends about the passing girls and their hunger for all things Pretty Committee–related. "I thought we weren't going to mention the date-ditch in public."

"It's not like people won't find out," Claire mumbled, her eyes swollen and red. "Besides, everyone's been staring at us all morning."

"Puh-lease, they're always staring at us." Alicia lifted her chin.

"I know word will spread, but as long as the Briarwood

boys are over there"—Massie pointed south, where the boy's school was located—"and OCD is over here, we can spin the truth. Call them liars. Spread our own versions of the truth. It'll be easy."

"I hope so." Kristen sighed just as Strawberry, the faux redhead, and Kori, her bad-postured sidekick, walked by their seats, whispering.

"Trust me," Massie assured them. "Besides, I have a new life plan." She pulled out her PalmPilot and read her screen, taunting the others with her mysterious new credo.

"What does it say?" asked Alicia.

"Share," insisted Dylan.

Kristen and Claire leaned across the others to avoid being left out.

"It may not be for everyone," Massie teased. "It's probably something I should do on my own."

"No," they pleaded.

Allie-Rose and Sydney half-turned their heads to try and eavesdrop.

"Do you mind?" sneered Massie, rolling her eyes at her lack of privacy.

The girls slid down the back of their seats in utter shame. When Massie could no longer see the tops of their heads, she continued.

"As of May third, I—I mean, the Pretty Committee is on a strict boy fast."

"Ah-greed." Dylan gave her the thumbs-up. "I gained eight pounds with my crushes. That's like four pounds each!"

The girls snickered.

"No more thinking about boys," Massie continued. "No more talking about boys, and no more crushing on boys." She paused for objections but there were none.

"We must rid our systems of all the boy toxins that are clogging our pores and dulling our complexions. So what if we're the Cheetah Girls. We don't need—"

"Um, question." Alicia raised her hand. "Does this mean I can't IM Josh tonight while I'm studying?"

"Not if you want to be part of the *New* Pretty Committee."

Alicia bit her lower lip.

Massie secretly held her breath while Alicia chose between a boy and her friends.

"Okay, I'm in." She removed Josh's Yankees cap and placed it gently at her side.

Massie exhaled. "Maybe the DSL Daters need boys to make them feel special, but we're better than that. We're *already* special. So from now on, the New Pretty Committee is boy-free. No more sadness, no more temptation. No more distractions. It will just be us, all the time, with clear skin, having the best time ever. Ah-greeed?"

"Ah-greed." They air-clapped.

"Done, done, and done," Massie nodded at her PalmPilot before shutting it off and dropping it in her gray Versace Madonna bag.

"Simmer down," grumbled Principal Burns as she bent the microphone closer to her thin lips and focused her beady black crow eyes on the students. "Simmer!"

The murmurs faded to whispers, which faded to a few dry coughs. And then silence.

"In preparation for summer, all lockers should be cleaned out no later than Friday at noon. I want all the stickers, mirrors, photos, and glitter letters scraped off the metal." She paused, giving way to the inevitable chorus of agitated mumbles. "If, at twelve-oh-one, so much as single shiny fleck catches my eye, everyone in that row will start off their summer break with a weekend detention."

More mumbles. A few random stares from LBRs looking to see how the Pretty Committee was reacting to the news assured Massie that even if word about the date-ditch had spread, she was still their beloved alpha.

"For those of you *not* spending this summer at five-star camps, yachting through the Mediterranean, or sunning yourselves on a beach in the Hamptons—the extra-credit summer school sign-up sheet is posted outside my office. There are several exciting new math programs to pick from, so take your time reading through the course descriptions before choosing."

The New Pretty Committee peered over at Kristen, who, thanks to financially challenged parents and a scholarship to uphold, would be all over that sign-up sheet. She kept her eyes forward, though, as if it had no relevance to her whatsoever.

"And now"—Principal Burns tucked her wild gray Albert Einstein bob behind her ears—"I have some terrible news."

The creaking-wood sounds of girls shifting in their seats echoed throughout the auditorium.

Massie's heart started to race. She loved a crisis. Loved watching people get all worked up about things. It added excitement into her life, especially when the crisis had no effect on her, which this ah-bviously didn't. Besides, it would be fun watching someone else in turmoil for a while, because she had certainly had more than her share in the past year.

She had dealt with Claire moving to town, Alicia trying to start her own clique, Nina the big-boobed boy-snatcher visiting from Spain, her first kiss with Derrington, getting expelled from OCD, watching Claire land the starring role in *Dial L for Loser*, searching for the key to a secret bomb shelter, prying it away from Layne, fixing up Chris and Skye, and wondering if Derrington would ever like her again.

And now, finally, with the creation of the New Pretty Committee, it was all behind her.

Principal Burns cleared her throat. "This morning, at three a.m., something devastating happened at our brother school."

Massie half-smiled. She was right. It had nothing to do with her.

"Somehow, the main water valve that was used to fill the wave pool was punctured."

Massie's palms began to itch.

Alicia fanned her face.

Claire bit her nails.

Kristen opened and closed the Velcro straps on her gray-and-black Pumas.

Dylan started chewing on one of her red curls.

And Layne, who was two rows in front of them, slid down in her seat.

"Two hundred and fifty thousand gallons of water gushed onto the roof of Briarwood and the old building." Principal Burns swallowed. "Well, the old building, she just couldn't handle the weight." Tears welled in her eyes. "And she collapsed."

Everyone gasped.

Principal Burns dabbed her wet, beady eyes with a crumpled tissue she'd plucked from her tweed blazer pocket. "And now the institution no longer stands as a New York State landmark. Instead, it looks like the lost city of Atlantis."

"We are so dead," Alicia mumbled.

"If we're lucky," Kristen mumbled back.

"I'm never lucky," moped Claire.

"Does that make us dead or not dead?" asked Dylan.

"Shhh," whisper-warned Massie. "You sound guilty."

"We *are*," Kristen insisted.

"No," Massie muttered from the side of her glossy mouth. "Layne is."

"Be assured that we are doing everything in our power to find out what caused this tragedy. And we are consulting with several European contractors about building restoration. But it's a long process, and it could take several years."

"Ehmagawd," Massie whisper-panicked.

"Ehmagawd," the New Pretty Committee whisper-panicked back.

Massie imagined her summer. No lazy afternoons by the

pool or vigorous rides on woodsy trails with Brownie. Instead, she'd be sweating in a stuffy orange jumpsuit picking trash off the side of Interstate 287 with the New Pretty Committee. It served her right for trusting *Layne* Abeley.

Principal Burns finally stopped talking, and Massie's ankle started shaking. She needed to get out of there and discuss, pronto. But instead of dismissing them, Principal Burns looked toward the back of the room and nodded once. The sudden pump of the door handle caused every head to turn.

A rush of overenthusiastic Briarwood boys swarmed inside, scanning the seated girls with the hunger of released convicts. They slid into any and all available seats, and even plopped down on a few of the eighth-graders' laps. No one had any idea what was happening, but the gleeful expressions on their faces proved they didn't care. There were guys in OCD. And this was more rare than a Louis Vuitton Panda Pochette special-edition handbag.

Massie, on the other hand, felt invaded and violated by the enemy.

"So please, give a warm OCD welcome to next year's new students," announced the principal with a mix of generosity and fear.

"What?" Massie jumped to her feet in protest. *"No!"*

Alicia jumped up too and applauded. Everyone followed except the rest of the New Pretty Committee, who looked up at Massie, waiting to be told how to feel about this shocking development.

"Sit down!" Massie grabbed Alicia's arms and lowered them both back into their seats. "This is bad. Very bad."

"Ehmagawd." Alicia quickly took her seat. "I totally forgot we hate boys."

Massie rolled her eyes, trying to downplay the giddiness that was swirling all around them.

Snippets of lively conversations danced in the air like the dust particles from moments ago. And everyone except the New Pretty Committee seemed to be taking part in them.

". . . do you think he'll sit at our lunch table?"

"We should start doubling to school. You can ride on the back of Jesse's bike and I'll ride on the back of Luke's."

"We *have* to go shopping."

"And tanning."

". . . he's the one in the black Lacoste—no, don't look. . . . He's totally checking you out. . . ."

"Can I look now?"

"No . . . wait . . . okay . . . now."

"Ohmygoshhe'ssocute!"

"Ehmagawd!" Massie gasped for air. "Do you realize it's been, like, an entire minute since anyone's even looked at us?"

"Huh?"

"It's like the boys are the new alphas!"

But no one responded. The New Pretty Committee was too busy scanning the crowd for their ex-crushes to notice much else.

"Is Olivia Ryan talking to Cam and Derrington?" asked Alicia.

"Yup," scoffed Kristen.

"I think I'm going to barf." Claire lowered her head in her hands. Her shoulders shook.

Suddenly Massie was overcome with flu-like symptoms. Her first instinct was to flirt with other guys, but as the founder of the New Pretty Committee, she couldn't. Which left her feeling embarrassingly helpless and lost.

"Ehmagawd, if Olivia so much as talks to Josh, she's dead to me."

"Kemp and Plovert won't even look at me," Dylan whined.

"Neither will the LBRs," Kristen gasped.

"Ehmagawd." Massie fanned her face with a musty prayer book. "What if our ex-crushes are the new eighth-grade alphas and we're the new . . ." Her voice trailed.

"The new *what*?" Asked Alicia.

Massie opened her mouth, but all she heard was a collective gasp from the New Pretty Committee. No further explanation was needed.

While the auditorium was buzzing with excitement and anticipation as the OCD girls and Briarwood boys mixed and mingled, Massie, Alicia, Kristen, Dylan, and Claire sat motionless. Their futures were clear. Their fate was obvious. And it could be summed up in three letters.

Three letters that would haunt them over summer break.

Three letters that would become their eighth-grade nicknames.

Three letters that would mark the end of an era.